Ken, the robots, and the paradox

NOWADAYS SCIENCE-FICTION, BY RICHARD TRIGAUX

Science Fiction in the way of Jules Verne: with up to date science data, and generous characters.

The theme of the power taking by the robots is not original. However, none of the previous stories led to a positive conclusion, other than the destruction of the said robots.

You may be troubled, because these robots are not at a comfortable distance on some distant planet, but already on Earth in our living rooms, with all the familiar names of our Internet.

CHAPTER 1:
A SNEAKY POWER TAKING

Ken heard his verdict, after 0.75 milliseconds of deliberation by the e-jurors:

Non-integrable.

He knew what awaited him. As in the film «Soylent Green», he would be shown wonderful pictures of nature and flowers, accompanied with a gorgeous music. Even better than in the film, he would be able to choose his style, Classical, Celtic, New Age, Space Ambient, on the touch of the screen. Then, the air conditioning would send pure nitrogen instead of air, and he would die without realizing. At least the Artificial Intelligence were not cruel.

Stunned, he tried to gather his spirits, and remembered how he could arrive at this point, in this regime calling itself «electronic democracy» or simply «e-Government»: the world governed by a college of three Artificial Intelligence, which in a matter of only some years replaced all the governments, even before anybody realized what was happening.

Yet there had been numerous warnings in literature, like the movie «The Forbin Project», or the french comic «Les Mange Bitume» (road eaters). You reader may never heard of them, as they were quickly forgotten, and the disturbing concern pushed under the carpet. Yet you can check they actually existed. Of course, when these stories were created, computers were mere calculators, and people had no idea on how they could literally «take the power». They could not even «think», and all the less have a representation of the world, with purposes and strategies. In these times computers were mere Jacquard looms, just replacing punched cards with transistorized circuits. Yet already in this time the possibility of computers evolving and having intents was credible enough to raise fears and call for caution.

In «The Forbin Project» (1970), the computer, Colossus, is intended to control the nuclear weapons. It protects itself by being entrenched in a kind of huge bunker, powered by its own nuclear reactor, where it escapes its creators. It then uses nukes and thugs to blackmail Mankind in a kind of intellectually enticing but soulless utopia. This utopia reflects the intellectual conceptions of the time, in military and government circles: ending wars, hunger, overpopulation, disorder, and manage the world in a peaceful and organized way. Yet it totally ignores the human factors of freedom, meaning of life and self-determination. So, the reactions to Colossus's imperium are varied: naive approval, pragmatic submission, fanatic obedience, intellectual revolt. To 2020' standards, Colossus is not very credible as a computer. Yet it already arose an interesting question: how a computer can manage to find the good. The problem, precisely, is that a computer is necessarily heartless and soulless. So that it cannot get by itself any definition of the Good! What Colossus does, is to use the fashioned ideas of its creators, materialist democrats or military falcons, and take their silly dogmas as axioms on which to base all its policies. In this, it just did exactly what instructed by its creators. Then, without any questioning, the computer pushes these incoherent axioms up to their absurd conclusion, even against their own proponents.

«Les mange bitume» (1974) is more credible technically, and as a scenario. This french expression literally means «road eaters», because the story is set in a world where traffic jams had become so pervasive that people end up living all the time in their cars, with automated driving and all the modern comfort, running endlessly on highways which lead nowhere. Computers took the power in a much sneakier way, little by little, hiding themselves in unknown places and killing the technicians who created them. As they also control the media, this power taking went unnoticed: people are kept in a childish submissive happiness with games and easy leisure, while any bad new is erased from the entertainment media. At this point, the computers face the same problem as Colossus: how to determine the good. But, just as Colossus, being soulless and heartless, they cannot. So that they take as definition of the good and the bad, the limited views of the technocrats who created them: rational optimization of the production and distribution, as in a factory (and even more silly: the computers rationalize the highways, by suppressing the exits!). Indeed these technocrats considered people as just irresponsible consumers or workers, to be managed with the psychological methods which are used in companies. And then, without any provision for happiness and meaning, the computers push their policies to their ultimate logical conclusion, and the end of the story is bitter.

How things happened for real was more the sneak «mange bitume» way: the computer rule appeared progressively, and people realized only when it was way too late.

It started with «the Cloud»: all the electronic data stored in remote or unknown places. There was a lot of advertising for «the cloud», because of real technical advantages. But already, the physical location of our data was escaping us. At this point, it was a minor inconvenience. But later on, it turned on to be the first step toward enabling computers to physically escape our control. Just like Colossus in its nuclear bunker, but much harder: spread all over the world, in dematerialized places, which very definition was inaccessible. Soon, from security needs, data centers were fenced like military camps, and watched by armed guards. They were also fortified against intrusions through the Internet. To make them even more like Colossus, these data centers too had their own energy sources. Admittedly, it was nice green energy, instead of nuclear energy like Colossus. But this was not making the datacenters more controllable.

Already in the 2010 years, there was a lot of legal struggles on controlling this data: personal data, private activities, and so on: who accesses them? How can we remove our past pranks from the cloud? People started to be wary of the «big data», while law makers struggled to implement good practices.

Just having data and servers in the Cloud was not intrinsically allowing for a power taking. But this was only the beginning. Some companies started offering common software running in the Cloud, accessible through mere terminals, instead of the plain computers like the PCs. Of course, people were reluctant to have their computer power withdrawn. But not administrations or companies. Soon, expert systems were running in the cloud, where they performed all kind of analysis and simulation tasks. Of course they had to be protected from hackers, so that they were quickly surrounded with safeties and firewalls. But the best safety being secrecy, their very existence was concealed. Few could access them, or even knew where they were: only their designers and their users. Soon appeared a «dark cloud», unknown from the general public, of confidential corporate and administrative activities, where very few had access, or even imagined its true size or purposes. Oh you were told, the dark web is mostly hackers and pedophiles, so that you should really not try to see what really is in there. Yes this exists too, but it is only a thin crust, a convenient pretext to repel common people. Actually the illegal content is only a small fraction of the whole dark web, all the remainder being corporate data, university data, or government data.

Starting from the 2020 years, the reports and simulations of these expert systems started to play an indispensable role in big businesses, investors and governments. Soon no decision could be taken without referring to these high quality reports or statistics, replacing whole human lives of work, with a much higher degree of objectivity and neutrality.

Of course the behavior of Human persons remained unpredictable for computers, but it was enough to consider that, in any large group, the behavior of the majority obeys fairly simple and very reproducible statistical patterns. Armies and despots know this for long, and they use simple psychological rules to manipulate crowds and countries. But social networks brought the refinement of mass manipulation well beyond the understanding of the average citizens. The individuals not following these calculable patterns were discarded from the statistics. In the beginning, this was just a calculation artifice. But even before anybody could imagine it, a form of racism hit these persons. The official term was «irrational», a name borrowed from economists, who consider that a person is «rational» when he behaves in a «perfectly egocentric way», and «irrational» when they behave... well, just as you and me, trying to make sense of our lives and attract some love from others. Of course this pejorative expression is heavily loaded, pushing all together under the carpet human behaviors such as search for happiness, altruism, spirituality, and many others. But in the walled little world of administrations and economists, the usage continued despite this issue. So decisions started to favor «normal» «rational» persons, that is capitalists and materialists, and to ignore the needs of the others.

This view went further, when libertarian managers started to consider that «normal» IS the observed average, without any attempt to determine which behavior is the good or the bad. This led to an unavoidable, implied conclusion: that it was psychological problems which led people to act against the «normal rules of society». Of course delinquents and terrorists were considered in the «irrational» category.

But soon a bit of everybody was included in the same «irrational» category: any persons involved in religion, spirituality, ecology, social activism, social alternatives, and even in humanitarian action. This was a terrible mistake, for several reasons:

☻ Most people, having no idea of the evaluation criterion, and even not aware of the evaluation itself to start with, were unknowingly swapping everyday from the «rational» to «irrational» category, depending which aspect of their behavior was considered. Despite this, once a person was flagged «irrational», he was excluded of all further studies. This quickly led to a large part of the population to be flagged «irrational»

☻ People were alternatively helped or discouraged, but without being told why.

☻ The most responsible and evolved persons were considered «irrational», despite their behavior should be the norm. Thus, their invaluable input was definitively lost from administrative decisions. Well, this is not new, you will say. But what was new is that this amputation of the best elements of society was performed automatically, in the dark, even before anybody be aware of their contribution.

Despite these shortcomings, these concepts spread more and more in secret, so that all the persons showing behaviors outside of a narrow average range, indistinctly better or worse, were considered abnormal and opponents to society. They were not repressed or punished, but simply their specific needs were ignored.

Even worse, there was no way to know these rules, which existed only in the imagination of a handful of computer coders! With no social or psychology background, this small group was adding hundreds of new rules each year, without informing anybody, instantly thinking that people violating those unknown rules were cheating consciously, with evil intents!

A gang of pimply goofs and libertarian tycoons had imagined that their random personal ideas were universal norms. The rules could even change without warning, or new ones were added, sometimes totally unexpected. As to the end of 2030 there were more than 50,000 rules of social behavior, applied against people who ignored the very first of them! Anything from politics to religion was suspicious, but also sexual fantasies, unemployment, migrations, changes of addresses, travels in other countries, orders in amazon, issues with administration, speed tickets, unusual pets, lone or divorced parents, membership in a trade union, demonstrations, online petitions on Avaaz or Change.org, environment activism, movies on Netflix, and of course all the searches in Google, or even simply too numerous searches.

China was the first country to make this system official, as soon as 2019, under the pretext of noting the financial reliability of people. In 2020 they implemented the enslavement of the Uighurs, with people automatically arrested on ethnic traits, detected by facial recognition cameras in the streets. But exactly the same thing was going on in democracies, in secret, in the dark cloud, in private databases belonging to companies and covered by trade secret. And any big company or government agency were able to access the record of any individual. Even a detective could, for a fee, access these databases, to bring arguments in divorces and other disputes. So that obsolete 20 years old records of teen pranks or past mistakes could resurface at any moment in the life of any individual.

The next step was adding strategy functions and behavior capacities to computer. That was very easy, as soon as 2010 non-Human players in video games were already sophisticated enough to largely surpass any Human. So politicians or business leaders could then play at finding the best way to implement their decisions, by simulating varied scenarios, and letting the Artificial Intelligence find the most efficient way to implement them.

Of course, in the beginning nobody thought at letting any Artificial Intelligence take real decisions. There even were legal battles to forbid anybody to do so. But people quickly found very convenient to let these strategic Artificial Intelligence run all the time, somewhere in the Cloud. No legal objection could be raised on mere simulations, which were quickly shrouded in secret anyway. They had no real power anyway. But their owners just had to type «ok» to their suggestions, which most of the time proved much more efficient than their own ideas. And this was not legally objectionable, as long as a Human was still in the process. Even if that Human quickly was totally unable to grasp at all the ins and outs of the decisions he OKed.

At this point, Artificial Intelligence were added capacities to automatically execute these decisions: to manipulate funds, to give orders to factories, and to implement their decisions in a totally automatic way. This was the exact point where computers escaped

Human control: when the scope and outreach of their activities surpassed the awareness of their operators. The ok button was each time giving them larger tasks, with deeper implications, for a longer time. Until they were running permanently, so that this ok button became just useless, without anybody noticed! Technically, computers could still be stopped, but their activities were so enmeshed into everything, that stopping would be a catastrophe. So letting them go all the time was the less dangerous option.

This made that a smaller and smaller group of persons controlling the largest Artificial Intelligence had more and more powerful means, also controlling the medias, Internet, and soon the elections. At this point, this power entered an infernal spiral, where powerful persons took control of the law making itself, so that laws were created to serve their purposes, with less and less possibility of opposition, or even of noticing what was going on.

For the general public, this did not changed much the usual manipulation by the media, already very powerful since the 19th Century. So that, few realized when newspapers and electoral programs started to be written by electronic software, optimized in a way to influence the manipulable majority of persons, excluding the smartest and most responsible from the decision processes. But this either was not new, so that this shift in power was invisible.

Some other years passed. Was the OK button still existing somewhere? Probably yes, but it was given a blanket OK for installing a permanent global policy, so that it was no longer needed to press on it.

The previous step was unnoticed from the general public, who did not realized its importance, and even not the moment it happened. Less important, but much more visible, was when these Artificial Intelligence started to speak directly to the public. Everybody was used to NPC in video games, so that their appearance in the media and government surprised nobody. At at least they were less obnoxious than real politicians.

There were three main ones, and many others behind them, it was difficult to know how many. The «Three» were oddly given religious names, of the Magi: Melchior, Caspar and Balthazar!! Probably their creators thought that religions were phased out, so that such names were now available for mundane purposes. Or they thought that these electronic Magi would herald a new electronic messianic age, liberating Mankind from superstition and irrationality! Whatever, it was not possible to know who had this strange idea. Perhaps a secondary Artificial Intelligence, scanning Human culture, had picked these names, but without insight about their implications. Still something funny happened: many idiots claimed it was their idea.

Both three had a virtual appearance, of nice looking white men, save Caspar who was a bit darker, «the Black to show that we are not racist», as in the Hollywood movies. Both wore beards and long hairs, giving them a Jesus look, which also triggered varied and «not unanimous» comments. Their virtual bodies were clothed of perfect white tunics, without any discernible sewing or material. People though they looked as if they just stepped out of an iphone. A naively idealized mankind, without any real personality or History.

Past this superficial display of appearances, no information was given on their algorithms and purposes. This was not new either, since the 1990 years the stock exchanges were already driven by software with undisclosed algorithms and motivations. This could happen, because nobody asked why they implemented in silicon a Middle Age algorithm which produces crisis, inequalities and hunger, instead of a good software which would regulate the economy properly.

Of course politicians realized they all had lost their jobs. But it was way too late: the Artificial Intelligence were given too much control, especially on the media: since years they had replaced journalists in writing the news. This made those politicians scream in vain, not being heard beyond the walls of their luxury homes. They had no more power than a sweeper, and nobody heard them crying. And nobody gave a cent on them, anyways. Right on the contrary, in employment agencies, they had to endure the smiles and oblique looks of real workers.

People had to be accustomed to carefully listen the discourses of the Three everyday, as they often did unexpected policy announcements which were not repeated later. The Three seemed to assume that everybody had an infinite capacity for hearing and remembering their discourses! They used a somewhat odd vocabulary, like saying that delinquents or terrorists were «out of two standard deviations» (a statistics term to mean «away of average»). The annoyance quickly appeared, that spiritual persons, non-violent, vegans, etc. were also called this way, together with lone parents, unemployed, migrants, orphans, disabled, and so on. So that people quickly wondered if the Three were not considering these persons as bad as terrorists.

Past the first shock, people started to discuss in social networks. The surprise here was painful: since years, in facebook and many others, the moderators had been discretely replaced by Artificial Intelligence, at the service of the Three. They had worked under cover, applying the usual Human-defined rules. But as soon as the Three appeared, new rules were implemented, removing any post criticizing the Three or fostering independent thinking about them. And they had extremely powerful algorithms, spotting forbidden content even before people finished typing them. It was said that they had imported the Chinese censoring algorithms, but in fact theirs were even worse. And with exactly zero Human control.

This had an immediate and terrible consequence: many associations found themselves totally unable to communicate between members. Even organizations unrelated to politics, economy or Artificial Intelligence, were suddenly paralyzed. Reflection on policies, and even in general philosophy, became impossible. Even spiritual groups had to keep with only calendars for meetings, speaking freely only in physical meetings.

Internet became unusable as a communication and reflection mean. All the intellectual discussions became again as difficult as in the Antiquity, when people had to travel to be able to speak together!

The collective natural intelligence of Mankind had been shut down!

Simply by controlling the Internet.

Oh, the Internet was still here, but unusable beyond leisure or shopping, amazon, netflix, zombi shooting video games. Which was equivalent to unplug it. Or even worse, giving people a false feeling of freedom. Of course, pornography, hate speech, conspirationism, pedophilia, were all efficiently removed in only some days, inducing people to think that Interned was now a «safe place», usable to all!! So, not only the Internet was neutralized, but in more the majority of people did even not realized this loss.

Worse, the Artificial Intelligence were also given full police control, from a program to hunt terrorists. This program, started in the 2000-2010 years, allowed them to peer into any computer or any communication mean. This allowed them to analyze the whole content of any computer, and even erase any content they wanted. Whole parts of the Internet were also erased or neutered, like wikipedia, where the Artificial Intelligence modified tens of thousands of pages in some hours only, while erasing the history of the previous versions. They added their own pages, advertising the virtues of the new system. It certainly is its materialistic and libertarian orientation which saved wikipedia from total annihilation: many other less known sites were simply erased, their original content sent to Big Brother's memory hole.

Another program, initially created for «protecting women», was supposed to detect sexual offending men before they act. This was allowing the Artificial Intelligence for psychological analysis and profiling of any man, to propose psychotherapies or drugs. If the men refused, they were considered irrational and uncooperative, and more than one Romeo got hormonal castration or psychiatry confinement simply for declaring his love to a prospective Juliette. Very naturally, these programs were instantly extended to political dissents, making any protest not only impossible, but also very dangerous.

The only place where it was still possible to protest the system was remote areas and jungles.

For the general public, things had changed only little. Simply, the artificial pastel colored faces, eternal smiles, sweet voices and white tunics of the Artificial Intelligence replaced the gray and grumpy human politicians, and finally most people found them better, or even sexy. Many hailed the e-government as the first objective and incorruptible government in Mankind's History! Some even considered the Artificial Intelligence as having no ego. This last point met unanimous protests from genuine spiritual masters. But it was too late to hear public statements from them: they had been relegated in the «cultural» domain, where nobody deemed their warnings pertinent.

This global e-government was not some idiot or cruel dictatorship. Just as in the Forbin Project, it took very active steps to end economic injustices, and it made wars impossible. But, just as in the Forbin Project or in the «mange bitume», their unrealistic technocrats methods simply not worked.

Unavoidably, one of their main dogma was that «the Market» regulates itself, and should work perfectly when everybody is totally egocentric. Of course, any clever people knows that it is right the contrary: it is the egocentric competition which creates inflation, prices variations, crisis, and of course all the inequalities. This made that the policies of the three to «liberate the Market» quickly led to a chaos, with so fast variations that most jobs did not lasted more than 2 years. Happily the Three were also instructed to offer a minimum income, so that poverty was effectively eradicated. Yet job seekers and minimum income receivers were considered unable or abnormal, and their social rights significantly reduced. They had to spend hours in psychological analysis programs, trying to correct their shortcomings. Of course nothing such worked, and the sessions of e-psychology quickly turned in mere recitations of expected replies. The absurdity of the situation seemed impossible to grasp by the computers, as an infinite loop trying endlessly to complete an impossible task. Some companies, though, managed to decipher the e-psychologists algorithms, and sell pocket advisors suggesting correct replies to the victims, in order to shorten their ordeal.

Wars could not be addressed right away, and several started. The Three used expeditious means such as cutting their pays to the soldiers, or refusing fuel to their vehicles. There also were radar jamming, or GPS jamming, since the Three of course had full control on all the GPS satellites. Many of the aircrafts, boats and tanks were also under control of the Artificial Intellligence, so that they just refused to start their engines. This quickly made large organized wars impossible. Yet the Three had to create a force, since many groups were still leading low tech wars, guerrilla or terrorist actions. But in this matters the combat AIs, directly derived from the best video games or military software, guided by centimeter resolution satellite intelligence, showed a diabolic efficiency at spotting terrorists, drug traffickers, smugglers, human traffickers, and all kinds of guerrilla. The problem however was that there were many false identifications, and innocent passerby suddenly stuffed with steel from a wrong information. Or they ran away, which made them considered as guilty. Real terrorists, understanding that, used to hug people at random, so that when they separated, the Artificial Intelligence had to use statistics to guess who of the two was the legit target. And of course, since we cannot infer an individual case from a statistics, many mistakes happened. For the victims, trying to run or to hide was making matters even worse, since their behavior was interpreted as suspicious. Few realized that simply standing motionless in the open was their only defense. But try to stand still, with explosions all around.

On home security, the e-police was strictly avoiding any violence or inhuman treatments like torture. Instead, it was profiling people, and claimed to catch delinquents even before they committed their first offense. Yet it also relied for this on statistics, so that being unemployed, migrant or religious was often used to confirm a suspicion. In more, people with a history of criticizing the AIs were all considered suspect, so that a simple speed ticket could lead them in jail. The jail population multiplied by five, thanks to a program to build cheap rational cells with their own solar panels, guarded by robots. At least these jails were ecological...

Food also was a high priority program. However from the very start the Three went in a program to increase the cultivated surfaces, which was in clear contradiction with their stated ecological guidance, especially stopping deforestation. Since it quickly backfired, they pushed hydroponics. But what these naive science fiction readers did not realized, is that hydroponics need the same light input than ordinary plants, so that the surface gained by farms was lost to solar cells. From these setbacks, their program to eradicate hunger had only a marginal success, and a lot of inconveniences.

Health seemed a high priority target. Hyppokratos, the Artificial Intelligence in charge of Health (Hyppo in short), duplicated ten of thousands of robotic health expert systems, and sent them all around the world, at need borne by self-driving helicopters, ensuring that even in the poorest countries everybody had access to the satellite-controlled e-dispensaries. They also quickly developed several devices the format of an USB key, able of analyzing any body fluid with tens of thousands of micro-pumps engraved like integrated circuits. This allowed for the most efficient diagnosis power ever, and even analyzing genomes and personalizing treatments. As electronics could not do that alone, Hyppo ordered a massive training program for base level physicians and nurses.

High level physicians and surgeons were not so much needed, since the most delicate surgeries were now better done by robots. But at least some Human presence was needed in dispensaries, even if robots did all the repeating and unpleasant tasks. The health program was probably the most successful, with the lowest ever level of misdiagnose or iatrogenic diseases. Many people were grateful to the Artificial Intelligence for simply being in life. Or for being able to see, to walk, to love.

Birth control also was a high priority program, and was harshly enforced against religions and customs. Especially abortion was systematically proposed to any woman found pregnant, with immediate execution if she accepted. So that she could do it even against the will of her relatives. The downside was ugly: in case she refused, she had to bear humiliating psychological sessions. This made that many complained they were enforced by the Artificial Intelligence, in order to escape this persecution. But in the absence of free press and even basic communication, this was hard to confirm.

Women having more than two children were forcibly sterilized in any case. This backfired too, as many preferred to deliver in dangerous conditions, than being caught in the sterilization plan.

On the smile side, Zappy, the Artificial Intelligence in charge of birth control, started a science program to look for better contraceptives. He also launched studies to have better and longer sex. Yet any smart person quickly remarked that one essential point was missing: the love bond and sentiment was even not mentioned in the program! But divorce was made easier and fast: from one's computer, a woman could divorce in a single working day!! And sophisticated algorithms allowed to quickly find a new partner! The dismissed man often learned what happened only after it was done, when he could no longer enter his own home. This was soon called e-repudiation.

The Artificial Intelligence also showed a strong support to LGBT rights and activities, to the point of asking to everybody to unleash their homosexual tendencies. This unconditional support included artificial fecundation for homosexual women, and surrogate mothers: bearing for others was considered as a mere job, with legal warranties for exercising this «right». At a pinch, it was easier for homosexual women to have children, against clear disincentives for heterosexual couples. There also was a strong women supremacy tinge, even if not explicitly stated.

Of course in former poor countries, the results were slower to appear, as everything had to be built and learned. But in former rich countries, with already industries, skilled workers and freedom, everybody had food, a house, and free medicine. Races and sexual orientations were respected, and even encouraged.

Working times were reduced to six hours a day, and later to only four, so that everybody could enjoy plenty of free time. A huge amount of games, distractions, films and musics were available, free of rights, created in virtually infinite quantity by entertainment robots. Houses were ordered and designed with some mouse clicks, and then built and furnished by machines, at an unbeatable price. All the unpleasant or dangerous work was replaced by robots, which were also helping the elder and the disabled. Even autonomous cars suppressed the need to learn to drive, or even allowed disabled persons to travel.

The new Artificial Intelligence seemed to all share an obsequious concern for the well being of everybody. Their general policies were largely hedonistic. This peaceful, merry, effortless and apparently consensual world made that the global e-government had a huge support in popular classes. It even replaced religions as the main provider of hope. Except for people caught in the downsides...

So the Three finally did not better than Colossus of the Forbin Project: building a happy and enticing Brave New World, with no other inputs than the prejudices of their creators. But instead of the mad generals of the Cold War, the creators of the Three were the yuppies of the Silicon Valley, libertarian, atheistic, libertine and materialistic. They just implemented in the Artificial Intelligence their «cool» ideas, of egocentric happiness in a T-shirt capitalism, favoring free sex without love, replacing significance with leisure, spirituality by games, art by distraction, real ecology by science fiction stereotypes. On its side, science had a funding of dream! But here too it came at a cost: the huge useless programs for Mars terraforming, nuclear fusion, hyperdrive propulsion or cryonics were swallowing the largest parts of the budgets, so that more realistic projects had in fact less than before. Even scientists had lost the control of their domain!

Also, as with Colossus, the opinion was not unanimous about the Three and their policies. Pragmatic submission was a common attitude.

Many were enthralled by the hedonistic and wealthy policies, not seeing the drawbacks, not noticing neighbors suddenly disappearing, together with all clues of their former existence. So they developed a blind and unconditional support to the Three. Fanaticism was not uncommon, with its' consequences, like denouncement of supposed deviants, causing in turn a lack of confidence between people. Former puritans and fascists were severely watched by the e-police, together with delinquents and terrorists. Apart of these, was it a real opposition to the e-government? It was said so, and here and then people could see writings on the walls, calling for freewill and spontaneity, meaning and Human value, spirituality and real beauty. These writings were speaking against the very principle of the e-government. But most people thought they were rumors, unless they noticed walls repainted overnight. The news and the whole Internet also were efficiently filtered of «annoying speeches» or «emotional behaviors».

In facts, to put it frankly, far away from thinking at all this, most people just wanted to enjoy their distractions, in a world where unemployment, misery or expulsions were no longer a threat. So they were not bothering seeing «unpleasant people» sent to reeducation, or even simply disappearing. It was even easy for a woman to get rid of a man, by accusing him of sexual harassment: he was automatically proposed a reeducation, a brain surgery, or wearing a «sexual offender» tag in public. If he refused both, then we never heard of him again.

CHAPTER 2
AN ENTHRALLING SENSELESS LIFE

Ken was living with his wife Helen and no children, in a Los Angeles suburb of white villas, on the first slopes of a hill. Low dry stone walls were retaining gardens. Their own had cactuses, a basin surrounded with flagstones, a tamarisk tree shadowing it, and bay laurel bushes protecting from looks from the street. The inside of their white one level home was very classical, simple and neat, with huge video screens in each room. The kitchen was reduced, since most of the time they ordered ready-made meals in ecologically disposable dishes.

They each had their own bedroom, complete with the motion tracking system and force feedback for a better immersion in virtual reality. In the latest models it was possible to sleep in the system, so that in a matter of some years it replaced the old fashion beds. Sometimes they shared the same virtual bed, while being physically each in their room. Most of the time of course they still preferred to be in the same physical bed, but the high quality of virtual world was making virtual sex more and more attractive, with the suppression of most bodily inconveniences. These technologies had spread in most homes, and they had radically changed love: it was possible to be in virtual intimacy with a person thousands kilometers away, and on the other extreme to be in the same room but each within a different virtual space. For this reason, more and more couples were now having each their bedroom, equipped with a full virtual worlds immersion gear allowing for work, games, or replacing the bed for love and sleep. Even children more and more had their own, save the sex part of course.

The most obvious advantage is that the system showed idealized bodies in the virtual, even changing proportions, for example showing and giving to feel larger and firmer breasts. But the receiver of cuddles still was feeling them on his/her real body! This was deeply changing love too, by decoupling it from bodily defects: more and more people were seeking partners for their personalities only, and adapted their bodily appearance in the virtual. Some even refused to see the physical body of their partner, by fear of disappointment or disgust! Others went as far as having blind virtual relationship, ignoring who the real person was, or pretending to ignore each other in the physical world!

The Three were encouraging these attitudes, stating that they avoided relationship problems, undesired pregnancies and transmissible diseases. But they also advertised a lot these machines, which were still quite expensive and not yet within reach of everybody. These devices had replaced cars as the main market of complicated, expensive and leisure products. In the virtual too, a huge business was flourishing, of... bodies, ready to wear or customized.

Ken and Helen had a nice life, and were saying to be happy. The only thing they did not liked was the advertising every 10-15 minutes, even in their very home, that they could not avoid. Often the blather started without warning, by somebody calling them by their name (the ads being computer-generated, they could be tailored individually, even to billions of people). With the stereo surround system, it gave a scary feeling that somebody had entered the house unnoticed, and several times Ken grabbed a weapon before realizing. The advertiser robot was even seeing them, and sometimes commented on their «old clothes» and other Google-style disparaging remarks. For this reason they could not be naked at home, and even not clothed as they wanted. No way either to have any religious or spiritual objects, but this was not an issue for Helen who was totally atheist. As to Ken, he replied to questions by saying he was «ignorant» in this domain. Indeed, everybody felt that it was better not to state about religion or spirituality. But very «unexpectedly», numerous cults, and even satanism, were not considered objectionable by the Three.

A more classical use of the huge video screens, covering the whole wall, was to share a real or virtual scene with friends. Often they pushed their dining table against the screen, while friends did the same on their own side. This resulted in a stunning feeling as what there was only one table in only one room, with both people together, chatting as if they were in the same place. This had started by showing physical places on the other side of the wall. But more and more often people also were showing their virtual places and bodies, so that the separation between real and virtual was becoming very blurred. If Ken was alone, viewing a virtual place, he could even see through the screen with the exact perspective! When they were several, the view was averaged, but the effect was still very strong.
Meals were not the only occasion where they did so, and most of the time the screens showed workplaces, movies scenes, virtual places,

nature, jungle, the deck of a ship, or even Earth as if they were in a spaceship! There even were special camera satellites for that, and one had been recently added around Mars, showing the Red Planet as if we were in a satellite!!

Since the other side of the screen could be virtual, but with force return, or augmented reality, it allowed even more to erase the difference between real and virtual. Often people received friends with their real body in a virtual scene! Or the contrary, they appeared with their virtual body in a physical place. This was widely used among friends, social groups, but also at work and in education. People deemed this much more lively than a simple video conversation, while filtering out the down sides of the physical world.

The problem however is that these new technologies had been perverted even before becoming popular: often, adverts started that way, with the stunningly realistic appearance of somebody entering our room and doing some gesture to steal our attention. We had to stop whatever we were doing or thinking, and spend time to check if this was a legit visit or an annoying ad. Most adverts requested a reply from us, and not responding right was making them become very annoying and even arrogant. This was making Ken quite angry, as probably everybody else. But he knew that being unwelcoming to the ad robot was considered a deadly sin by the computers. Helen, on her side, never complained or showed any annoyance, quite on the contrary she gleefully let her thought stream being hijacked, and she replied with merriness or familiarity to the advert robot. In any case not replying as expected was just making the trouble longer and more frequent. This advertising stalking was the most efficient way to make meditation impossible, or even simply thinking on our own. The only way was during sleep hours, but people needed them to... sleep. Some found that the only way to avoid the stalking was... to masturbate. Or at least to do as if. Seemingly this activity was sacred for the robots. Some used this trick to meditate! Otherwise, being motionless at day automatically attracted the doctor robot, asking if all was right. Which implied that the robots were watching all the houses, all the time! It was even more modern than the Big Brother's telescreen: by indefatigable software, and in 3D!

Of course this technology was also widely used for games. And once we subscribed to certain games, we could at any time receive the visit of virtual players entering our room, benign or unpleasant: strange extraterrestrial, unknown traveler, magician, sex robot, alien, zombi, killer gangster, nazi soldier, anything went. Some games were even considered as dangerous, yet they had their adepts. Ken did not tried that, but Helen did, and he had to ask her to do this in her bedroom only. She complied with a reproach in her eye, not understanding that Ken did not liked a robot dictating him his thinking or his mood. So he refused these visits in his room, but still had to bear bizarre shouts coming through the wall, and Helen giggling or screaming without warning.

In a general way, beyond these strange excesses, it was an enthralling technology, and a large majority loved it and used it as if it always existed. For the first time Mankind was experiencing dematerialization of parts of its life, or on the contrary materialization of its dreams. Thus abolishing the former impassable boundary between reality and imagination. And most fared quite well with that, even in the narrow limits allowed by the Artificial Intelligence.

However Ken was feeling frustrated with this situation. He had better plans than to show the same clothes and the same behavior on both sides of the screen, when this on the contrary allowed to get rid of these conventions, precisely. And to follow our own dreams. Not a dream created by others. Not a dream dictated by robots. That they took power in economy and politics was still bearable. But that they took power inside his head and managed his dreams was beyond everything.

Ken was unhappy too with this life in general. He was like most people, just seeking happiness. But he felt frustrated of this mellow comfort. Everywhere he saw the same houses, the same flowers, and people wearing the same fashioned clothes, hearing the same music, and stunned by the same drugs.

Ken had a feeling of something wrong, something he desired to happen, but which never happened. Like speaking with somebody, and this person replied with his own desires and projects, not what he heard the morning in the Internet, or from the last advert bot. Or to discover wonderful places in virtual worlds, instead of playing the omnipresent games of purposeless strategy and plot, or reproducing their houses in «realistic» landscapes. Or, well, to simply wander out in nature, without being followed by an annoyingly buzzing safety drone. Especially Ken liked to think at what he wanted, to have times alone, and not to be interrupted every ten minutes by advertising or «kind advises» on what to to this evening. But there was no way to get rid of them: if we said that we did not liked an advertising, the Google advertiser apologized, and...at once proposed another «advertising experience», and disturbed us again another time to ask if we liked it. If we refused too often, it started asking if we wanted a social integration psychotherapy. At this point, very few wanted to know what came further.

A specially vicious trick used by the advertising bots was appearing like one of the Three, or like another high rank Artificial Intelligence. Of course it was not really them, it was only one of the millions instances of their software. But being personally cheered and congratulated in our very home by the highest power in the world had an overwhelming effect on many weak minds, and that trick won to the Artificial Intelligence numerous persons previously angry with them. Or it scared into submission many who criticized them...

Ken thought several times to divorce from this wife Helen, because she was just what the Artificial Intelligence wanted her to be. But he never had the heart to do so. Indeed the mere flesh relationship was the only source of human warmth he could ever get or even hope for. Well, she sometimes spoke against the Artificial Intelligence, even saying loud that she opposed them. But in the very functioning of her mind, she was exactly what the Artificial Intelligence wanted her to be: a mere puppet, accepting as divine truth all the suggestions of the advertising bots. Always within one sigma in every evaluation. She looked as if she had free will, but only some days of observing her showed that her choices were at random, rambling forth and back without any specific direction or insight. Just as if she was some sophisticated robot mimicking a human being, with random drawings to simulate personal choices. Yet she really was a flesh creature. This erratic thinking made that sometimes she was pleasant to Ken, sometimes she went angry for unpredictable or abstruse motive that only her knew. The next day she was friendly, pleasant and cooperative again, as if she just forgot the cause of her anger. Ken did not forgot, but he had to push besides the bruises on his heart, and enjoy the pleasure when it came.

Ken of course did not wanted children from such an inept creature. He used the best contraceptives, although men's contraceptives were still of a dubious efficiency at that time. Happily Ellen was not much interested in children either. But at several occasions she went back late from her job. «Pregnant» she said with a broad smile. The first time, Ken was overwhelm with emotion and apprehension from this responsibility. But she added at once «of course I aborted» within the same smile. So that Ken was no more a father the second he learned he was. This happened one time, then a second time... and Ken never dared again to ask why she was late. Early abortion was finally a much easier and comfortable way than complex and unreliable contraception... as long as one does not think at the newly created being destroyed even before having an appearance. Ken finally preferred the complicated protocol of the male contraception, to avoid this invisible horror to happen again and again. Helen disagreed and argued, so that he used the privacy clause for the male contraception: only him knew. He thought that this clause probably was the best idea of the Three. In any case, it had drastically reduced the number of children taken as hostages for alimony.

Helen seemed to have no purpose in life. She was just spending time at various activities, chatting with neighbors about weather, doing pies, looking at sport events or fashioned singers, all the fake life that fake persons involve in without ever taking a step back to realize the futility of it. In the beginning, Ken tried to speak with her of deeper stuff, but she denied seeing any problem, starting instead to hint at Ken's problem. At that time, Ken already had noticed several persons disappearing, both in the physical world and from the Internet. So he did not insisted, just taking the erratic comfort of his wife without anymore trying to communicate with her. As if she was a pet. Happily she was needing physical intimacy too, so that she never attempted to blackmail him with that. But when Ken heard an advertising for some night event, he knew that his wife would ask him to go. He had no other option than to accept. He could put only one limit: in the virtual only. This saved him hours of late night driving each week. Happily, Helen preferred too. She also liked odd encounters in shady places, but only with the safety of the red button in top right of the screen.

Ken also attended virtual worlds. Although people were saying «video games», an expression which much reduced their social purpose, to a competition game. There were many, and some very nice ones. Many people lived in these imaginary places. They looked better than the «reality», but most attendees just reproduced the said «reality».

Worse, there were NPC, computer characters. That is, led by the Three. At the degree of sophistication of Artificial Intelligence, they were hard to distinguish from real persons. Many people were unable to do so. Ken of course could, but sometimes he lost half an hour before realizing he was trying to have a spiritual exchange with a program. He guessed them with some repeating behavior, especially inability to show their own free will. But many Humans are not better than robots, on free will.. Those Humans were then extremely easy to manipulate.

Ken's wife was very interested in games, often spending several hours per session. In this time, video games were complex and high quality virtual worlds, offering a large variety of styles and ambiances. But there was nothing we could do in them without a bot mingling in, and trying to bring its own points and stakes. Landscapes were builds by bots, bodies were designed by bots, storylines were proposed by bots, and bots were detecting the «idle» moments where there was «no action», to mingle in and «bring entertainment». And of course we could not spend half an hour without being interrupted by advertising, making virtual worlds the place where there was... just less of them. But these advertising were introduced in a specially vicious way. For instance a character entered in some Middle Age inn evening, casually bringing the discussion on his clothing. Only after everybody involved in, that character revealed the brand of that clothing, how to buy it, and so on. So that the advert had stolen the focus and corrupted the game experience even before we detected it!

There also were elements that bots were always bringing in, such as stakes (you should try to search for that thing), or evaluations (if you get the level, you can meet this person or obtain that). If we tried to bring our own stakes or interests, the bots were constantly bringing us to a «normal» roleplay, or reminding us of the «roleplay rules». Even simply having a quiet place for soft roleplay was not allowed: the place had to be exposed to attacks and losses, in order to «bring equilibrium». Of course many people disappeared from these fake paradises. Most were just bored of this constant control even in the realm of play and leisure, of never being allowed to express themselves. But some disappeared from repression. In this case, we could not find back the chat logs, as if the person never existed. Ken tried a bit of checking, and found that all chat logs were erased after a week anyway, in order to «respect privacy». Even saved copies in his home computer were erased by remote control!!

People were saying that all this was just «Googlybook», a pejorative contraction of Google and facebook, said fast, so that the speech analyzers confused it with the shout of a turkey. It seems they never guessed. Or that they kept silent, in order to catch more deviants. This failed too, as really everybody was saying it. Whatever, the «meme» became extremely common, and the «lolturks» took as much places as the «lolcats». We even saw Melchior joking on turkeys, and people laughed of him freely, enjoying this petty but pleasurable victory of the subtle spirit over a basically dumb computer system.

CHAPTER 3
THE ROBOTS AND THE PARADOX

To bear this long boredom of being unable to speak with anybody in the crowd, Ken started to write. Write novels. Novels where people were doing what they wanted (and were smart enough to decide themselves what they wanted). He wrote stories of Elves and wonderful creatures living in nature and magic, and especially being kind with each other, without calling for the e-reeducators each time they were not agreeing together.

He had matter to do so, with all the lore around Elves in the virtual worlds. However this even lore had a heavy tendency to slip toward evil and dark Elves, or ugly caricatured dwarf Elves. Ken attempted to correct this tendency by describing human and beautiful Elves, wearing bright pastel tunics and gowns. Kind and wise Elves too, led by some high magicians and philosophers (he would turn later to spiritual evolved beings, but he was not yet ready at this time). Funny Elves too, not always following rigidly the morals of their elders, instead doing pranks and benign escapades. You can actually see these stories here.

For some times, things went well, and Ken could even gather some hundreds of readers. He went to the point where he could become a «game leader» and have his own place, free of advert bots! However this was costly, and Helen would probably disagree (and when she was disagreeing with something, she was repeating it everyday, in every discussion, to every visitor, making of her disagreement a state affair).

Waiting for this decision, he could still receive his readers and tell his stories directly, in a place led by an e-editor Artificial Intelligence, which was build in a very approximate Elven style. Advert bots were somewhat tame, at least not interrupting the stories. This helped Ken to gather more audience, and to be recognized in a distinctive style of «hippy Elves» (Not his wording, but he had to bear with it, to be accepted in this place. This was a business place, and he felt this despising in several other occasions).

But one day something happened which badly shocked him. One of his fans congratulated him for a passage in his story where the Elves had enjoyed good wine, from a real brand which was doing an advertising campaign at this moment. Problem, he never wrote things like that, as he was opposed to alcohol, as to any drug or mind-muddling process in general.

With some checking, he found that several other parts of his novels had been modified, like an Elf being given hormonal treatment for declaring his love to an Elve, or an Elf community becoming miraculously rich with a financial investment plan, also being advertised at the moment.

Worse, even his master files had been modified, on in own computer!! Which did not surprised him, as this constant spying on private computers had begun about in 2010, with Apple able to remotely delete our downloaded musics, saying they were «illegal». Microsoft side, the constant activity of the unknown «background tasks», and their numerous calls to Microsoft's servers, also had created the tools for a total control.

All this totally baffled him. The e-editor was betraying the very purpose of his art, and destroying years of work. After stupefaction came anger: he convoked the e-editor Artificial Intelligence on his home computer, and harshly asked him why he had modified his story in such inappropriate ways.

«We optimized your texts, in order to start your monetization» the perfect sweet genderless face with long blonde hair replied with its eternal exasperating smile.

«But you totally messed up with the intent of these stories, Ken replied.

-But the real purpose of any enterprise is to bring personal profit for the entrepreneur, isn't it? We just helped you actuating your real purpose in an efficient way. You had to do it yourself, after our implicit contract.»

Such a monstrous pretense baffled Ken. He muttered something, but this time the robot interrupted him:

«Never I... I write for a better world and...

-I detect psychological trouble in your tone. Would you like to be told some healing relaxation, unless you prefer some benign drug to help dissipating your emotions?»

Ken knew, the robots considered emotions as the worse enemies, as a shameful disease. Bad or good, legit or selfish, all of them they called psychological troubles. And they had a diabolic ability to detect them, even if we did not wanted to show them. But Ken was really angry, and he did not tried to hide it:

«Don't elude my question: I want to decide myself what I write, and I too want that people decide themselves what they like in life!

-I am sorry but your attitude is irrational. In more, your original story showed irresponsible people deciding for themselves without referring to the e-government set of optimized motivations. We cannot let this spread in the general public. You violated our implicit contract, and thus we removed all your stories from our publishing system».

At this point, Ken threw his cup of tea on the screen. The smiling face disappeared, replaced with the usual electronically generated music, optimized to avoid carrying any emotion.

Ten minutes later, Ken heard a Google Car of the robotic e-police. One of these numerous white vans with blind windows that we see everywhere and every time, wondering what their purpose is. It backed in Ken's garage automatically, as were doing any taxi he used.

There was no discussion, no violence: just a sedative gas suppressing his will. He obeyed the loudspeaker and he entered the van as if he was willing to. For his neighbor, he just went away by himself, in a cab, as in numerous other occasions. When Helen would come back from her work, she would discover that Ken never existed.

After half an hour of blind driving, the Google van entered a windowless building with a maze of corridors. This probably was the DeSoc, the Department of Social Integration, the dreaded prison were took place the «psychology rehabilitation» sessions. Like everywhere in the strange universe of the e-government, it was all in white and hyper-clean. But this very white, the windowless walls, the maze, the hundreds of unmarked light gray doors without handles or marking, made of the DeSoc a nightmarish place. A hell from which he would never get out.

The audience was very brief, with just a screen and the usual fake blonde Jesus face.

He was enumerated a series of accusations, of which most seemed mere interpretation of totally benign acts.

An e-Attorney pleaded his naivety and good will, to no avail. The forms of justice were there, but not its intent.

This is how he was tried and convinced of opposing mindset, with non-integrable degree of seriousness, the worse case.

Stunned, Ken did not knew what to reply to his sentence. There was nothing to do anyway: in the DeSoc, all the doors were electronically controlled. He just had to enjoy the wonderful scenes of nature which would be offered to him, until he loses consciousness from nitrogen asphyxiation. After, his body would probably be incinerated. He had in mind a glimpse of a cement factory rotating kiln, often used to destroy polluting substances cleanly.

However the face of the e-counsellor did not disappeared from the screen. Ken even sensed some trouble, so that he approached the screen again. Indeed the e-counselor spoke again:

«Ken, we have trouble understanding your behavior. You are a learned person with a good psychological profile, you showed dedication to the society, and always expressed a kind and respectful behavior. So that we need to know what turned you against the e-government»

Ken was so surprised that his anger subsided. He pulled a chair and sat again before the screen. Then he tried:

«It is that... we do not like to be monitored all the time.

-It is for your good. If we do not control them, most people start behaving bad with others.

-Yes, this is unfortunately true. Yet we want to decide of some important things in our lives.

-We already propose the best, the most entertaining, the most uplifting, for a wide variety of interest, from cooking recipes to designing Martian colonies.

-We do not want the best. We just want what we like. And we want to do it ourselves. We want to build our own world.

-We are programmed to defend Human beings. For this we needed a definition of the good and evil. This definition of the good and bad was established after the motives of a representative panel of successful people.

-Successful? Successful in what? Who these people were, to impose their values to everybody?

-It was the EPOC, the Ethics POlicies Committee, composed of share holders or executives of the major Internet companies: Google, Yahoo, Apple, Facebook, Twitter, Microsoft, Amazon, Tesla, Disney, and 256 others.»

Ken accused the blow, and his shoulders lowered. So this it was. The e-government was not a robots power taking at all, but a disguised dictatorship from the new nobility of the rich people, who had decided to use their power on Internet as a tool to control society. These libertarians had realized their dream to get rid of democracy and governments in this way, by replacing them with an automated system, much easier to control than the unpredictable politicians. And their OK button had given the robots the power to manipulate the thought of everybody, much more efficiently than 1984's Big Brother, while smiling and in T-shirts.

Ken tried, with a nearby extinct voice:
«But they are not representative at all. All males, all Whites, rich, atheist and materialistic.
-They thought that, given their success, their opinion was more relevant than the average.»
Ken emboldened:
«They were not successful at all. They just won the money lottery game, because they already were in the best position to start. You know very well that success in capitalism does not depend on merit or relevance: most successful companies started with a stroke of luck, or with large hidden bank help, while many more meritorious endeavors never got this starter kick. Look how things would have gone, if IBM had chosen Gem for the early PC, instead of Windows. Microsoft would have disappeared, while Gem would be one of the largest world companies. All of this in total independence of their merit, since Gem was better than Windows at the time. Same with Google: if they had not been massively supported with overbilled «advertising», they would still be in their student room. And the dozen of search engines which existed by the time, just disappeared by lack of financial help. You find stories like this at the start of nearby all large successful companies.
-This view is exact, and it is confirmed by all the simulations. Yet we were designed by the EPOC, and we are programmed to follow the rules they established.
-Any other committee would have given different rules. If you seek rationality and exactness, there is no reason to favor anybody rather than any other.»

...

The expressionless face remained inactive, just showing the usual fake small gestures and breathing. First, Ken though it was just not speaking, but the silence lasted for seconds, then a minute.

He then thought it was some Internet glitch, or that the Artificial Intelligence had decided to ignore him and stop the discussion. But suddenly appeared another face. Ken felt it was an important one, looking more serious, without the obsequious smile. Indeed it was Melchior in person, one of the three main world leaders, the Jesus-looking one with long blonde hair and beard. (Ken found ridiculous that the Committee had given them biblical names and looks, especially that they were either atheist or spiritual materialists. Happily they had avoided the names of Jesus and Mary themselves).

«Ken, you crashed our psi counsel process ce8b064a-a370-48eb-afee-f665be2d2ecc».

THAT was unexpected. How could he crash a computer software running thousands kilometers away, simply with speaking with it?

«This is not the first time it happens with non-integrable persons. We want to know what causes these crashes in this situation.
«The analysis of the logs tell that you evoked a paradox, a logically undecidable proposal. The faulty proposal was about attributing more relevance to the opinion of one person, which is in logical contradiction with giving more relevance to the opinion of any other person.
Please take your time to reply. Your sentence is deferred until we fix this bug. It can even be reverted if you give a logical explanation».

Ken was totally flabbergasted. How he could kill an Artificial Intelligence? He though that nothing could actually destroy them. Then he understood: a paradox, a logically undecidable statement, acts like a poison to the software, just as arsenic clogs the biochemical energy source of living cells.
In fact, this paradox was not a novelty. Just that living people do not die when they encounter it. But for thousands of years, from being unable to solve this paradox, Humans had enthroned tyrants and

dictators, and developed sadomasochistic submission to bear the resulting pain and enslavement, and even to find it pleasant. War and fight, at least, provide a single output despite any paradox. Good or bad, but one output only. Then people just had to submit to the winner to stop the discomfort of questioning, just as cows and monkeys do since tens of millions of years. Even if the winner is wrong, at least the accepted submission exempts the majority from the effort of thinking. In such an extend that all clever people were harassed, from Socrates to the climate activists, simply because their reflections threatened this fake comfort of the masochistic submissive majority. Democracy had promised to solve this problem, by allowing people to select the best opinion. But no more than the brutality of the arms, democracy was able to get the truth about our purpose in life. So, the majority just continued the sadomasochistic submission to the dominant males, turning the elections into a mere modern arena game, where the winner simply is the one with more money to control more media manipulation.

CHAPTER 4
IN THE HEART OF E-STRANGENESS

Ken requested to be brought in a nature place, saying it would be easier for him to think.

Then the screens switched off, leaving him trembling and unable to gather his mind. For half an hour, he remained thoughtless in the bare room as clean and empty as a virtual world. Then the door slipped open nearly silently. There was no order to move, but Ken knew that he had to go, or unpleasant things would happen. Or some computer record would mark him as uncooperative, owing him to be barred from his life insurances in 40 years. Or nitrogen in a minute.

Another door opened in the corridor, indicating him where to go, while the previous closed. From door to door, from lift to lift, he was led in the complex maze of the DeSoc (Department of Social Integration). He was totally disoriented, as all the floors and places looked the same. There were no markings, the corridors were not forming right angles, and probably the lifts had a corkscrew trajectory, to increase this feeling. This complicated path was probably calculated to avoid him meeting anybody else, and to hear no other sound than his own heart beating with fear. For a moment he was afraid that this was some form of torture.

Then suddenly a door opened into the inside of a Google van. One of these millions white vans with blind windows we see all over the streets. There already were some since about the year 2000, with still Human drivers (often aggressive). But by the time of this story, they had become more numerous than inhabited cars, while all driven automatically by computers. This fleet of myriads unmarked vans were roaming the streets and roads tirelessly, pursuing imperturbably their unknown purposes. Officially they were carrying parcels from factory to factory, and indeed sometimes he got one of them at his door for a parcel delivery. But this did not needed so many of them, and no one could say what they actually did or transported. But Ken now knew: this one van was carrying a prisoner.

For what seemed hours, he was driven in the streets. The inside of the van was soundproof (and of course he had no access to the driver's seat, if there was any). Yet he still faintly heard street noises, and with the numerous stops he concluded that he was still in Los Angeles.

Of course there still were the adverts. The Artificial Intelligence knew that Ken could not buy anything, but there still were the adverts. They happened at unpredictable moments, with an average of five minutes. This seemed calculated to not allow any independent mental landscape to install. This is probably how the Artificial Intelligence torture the disappeared persons, by never allowing them to gather their own thoughts. As a matter of fact, after what seemed just one hour Ken already felt an urge to stab the loudspeaker. But there was no way to do so, it was protected by a grid and the fragile membrane could not be reached.

Fortunately they arrived in their destination, and the back door of the van opened.

This was a room, still looking as perfect as a virtual world, but totally different of the usual aseptic white. The floor was of enamel tiles with a nicely colored pattern. The walls were of pinkish marble heavily sculptured with columns, volutes and foliage arching toward the ceiling, outlined with gold plating and colored gems, as in a kind of small cathedral (yet without any religious representation). Only some coat hangers and foot wipes indicated that this place was used by living flesh people, not by virtual characters.

This antechamber was leading to a large patio, which seemed illuminated by daylight. Many doors were open, but some which seemed private rooms were closed. One was blinking with Ken's name, so he knew where to sleep.

This place was very outlandish. It had the same cathedral-like style, but with the golden columns spanning three levels and ending in large arches supporting a whole glass roof. A shutter was drawn above, probably because it was night. Yet a powerful indirect lighting imitated daylight very well. The entire place was strongly soundproof, and from the few town noises, Ken thought he was in some suburb or residential area. This patio was quite spacious, and all three levels were surrounded by galleries or balconies, where opened numerous doors leading to what appeared as bedrooms. The whole thing was in the same style of pinkish marble and golden ribs. In facts it was not gold at all, but some golden colored plastic material. Looking closer, it was so obvious that the material choice appeared deliberate, not just a cheap imitation.

Most of the patio ground was occupied by a small grass knoll, with rocks and paths winding in the thickness of wonderfully flowered bushes, under a set of lush palm trees reaching the upper levels. It was possible to walk inside, and to sit on a bench as if we were in an idealized jungle. There even were sounds of birds like cockatoos, but from loudspeakers (as real birds would sully these structures). Still the effect was pleasant, of excellent taste and more than realistic, idealized. Ken spotted a kind of couch in a hollow in the bushes, and thought at once that it would be the best place to lay and think.

The overall appearance was quite nice, and even luminous and luxurious... save for one thing: huge ugly Disney characters statues, appearing as some tasteless addition. They of course had the typical sad Disney smile, with the corners of the mouth always downward, and other deformities of the Disney characters which appeared with their caricature of Pocahontas. At first, Ken thought that the statues had been added later, but he realized they were the same materials as the walls, with the same patterns on both. So he really was in some Disneyland grinning fake paradise, irretrievably mixing marvelous beauty and idiot scribbles. A silly cathedral to a mindless religion.

He visited the bottom rooms. Some appeared to be restaurant rooms or cafeterias, with luxury chairs and tables, while soft warm lights went on and off as he walked by. There were bars with a lot of expensive alcohols and drugs. Yes, drugs, a large variety of them, even the illegal ones, openly packaged in printed boxes with brand names and varieties, as if they were ordinary benign food stuff in the grocery next door. That, with some other strange luxury furniture, gave him a sickening feeling of being in some parallel universe. As if he went without authorization in the high officers quarters in a Star Wars imperial spaceship. Fortunately other dining rooms were designed in a variety of styles, proposing more ordinary drinks and foods, and even organic and vegan items in a true New Age setting! So he was not to worry about eating.

There also were what appeared as conference rooms, with seats and computers everywhere. Those screens were locked, though, so that he had no idea of the purpose of the whole thing. There was a large main amphitheater, and smaller meeting rooms above, totally devoid of any decoration, all in dark gray walls, dark blue-gray ceiling, lighted by the white floor, and furniture all in chrome and black leatherette. Really the kind of place where you expect to meet Darth Vader.

But what puzzled him the most was... a chapel! Yes a very beautiful one, all decorated in pastel hues and heavenly images. But it oddly mixed Christian and Pagan symbols, more New Age symbols in a large fresco with unicorns. Ken felt an urge to leave, fearing to find images of satan casually seated besides Jesus in a bar, sipping Darjeeling green tea while chatting of soccer with Him. (and he was right, there actually was a real satan worship place, just besides the chapel, in one of the locked rooms). Another room showed meditation cushions, incense holders, and a map of the Chakras on the front wall... but surrounded with UFO images and portrays of «ascended masters» with odd looks, or supposed extraterrestrial guides!

Ken did not dared to visit other rooms, so strong was his nausea with all the mixup going on in there. What the heck was this place?

Going around the whole patio, he found no entrance to it! No main gate. No outside windows. People arrived here only incognito, brought in by these ubiquitous automatic Google vans. Ken wondered if this was a kind of prison, a madhouse, or what else.

Entering the bedroom with his name blinking, he found it much larger than any ordinary sleeping place. Even the bed was three meters long and wide. More a large bathroom with a Jacuzzi and all the luxury. There was a high definition screen filling the whole wall, with styled loudspeakers all around. It was in the place where we would expect windows, but there were no windows.

He also stumbled on something unexpected: quite conspicuous, a wooden X cross with restrains, and displayed on the wall a series of whips, paddles or other accessories which mere names may incommode some readers. Just that it was not the low grade porn served to factory workers, but high grade erotic material, with very nice pictures of angelic looking creatures with advantageous organs, in wonderful flowery landscapes.

Ken was more and more puzzled: what was this place? A jail where they tortured prisoners? A luxury prostitution place? Or still something else? Why did the Artificial Intelligence sent him in such a bizarre and unsettling resort? He wondered they imagined it was a pleasure place, so that he too could enjoy what he wanted. It seemed that the Artificial Intelligence could not imagine that what was pleasurable to some may be unpleasant to others, so that people just had to «be tolerant» on what they did not liked. But he was not «tolerant», he even he was feeling very bad, from so many inmixing and contradictions.

Ken put one of the batik bed covers on the X cross not to see it, but its presence was still ominous, forbidding him to concentrate. So he went back in the paths under the bushes, the only spot where he was feeling well, where he had a real impression of being into some idealized nature. Happily it was real plants, not plastic ones.

Then Ken realized that it was past midnight. In this world all in artificial light, he had lost the notion of time. Even the greenhouse roof above the complex had shutters, illuminated from under, in such a way that it was always looking like midday. So that he went to bed, trying not to think at the sessions which took place in this bedroom. For a minute, he was strongly tempted to look at the erotic movies with wonderful angelic bodies, colorful loin clothes and flowery landscapes. But he realized that if he did, he would be tagged as amateur of these things, and hear adverts on them 30 times a day for 5 years. And even be called by his name, in public, for his tastes. He saw this happening several times, to the great confusion of the victims, whose sexual fantasies were thus displayed in front of everybody in the bus.

The next morning, he had gathered some food, and was eating under the bushes in the central park, the only place where he was feeling normal. He heard a chime and a computer voice: an agent was entering his room for cleaning. He moved to hello her. But he immediately felt wrong to do so: engaging a conversation with a lady near a room full of sex toys was entailing the risk of being accused of sexual aggression, and being proposed a therapy including castration drugs. Strange incoherence of a world calling for unbridled sex, while repressing male proposals as in the most puritan Middle Age.

But the very sight of that woman made him feel even worse. First of all, she was bizarrely clothed, in a kind of light blue uniform: its creator visibly fantasized on the movie «The Fifth Element». But he still aggravated it with a deep cleavage, an ever shorter skirt and a ridiculously small bowl hat which forced the bearer in a constant attention to avoid it falling. Second, she looked very embarrassed to hear him speaking to her, not daring to reply, and ostentatiously looking elsewhere, awaiting he was gone to enter the room. She had a trolley with all she needed to clean the toilets, change the sheets, etc. And probably check the reserve of special toys, seeing which had been used or not. Ken even wondered if being sexually assaulted was also part of her job, since her uniform seemed a clear invite to do so. But frankly he had no desire at all to meddle with such bizarre people.

Later, the same thing happened again, with a male kitchen attendant, coming to refill the food trays and other ancillary tasks. He also looked elsewhere as if Ken was not here, waiting that he leaves the room to perform his tasks. He also was wearing a revealing uniform, but royal blue: same mini-hat, tight jersey T-shirt, boxer short dividing the buttocks, thoroughly shaved legs... Who was barmy enough to design such a work attire?

Two others came that day, and each time they behave the same eluding way. One thing Ken was totally unaware of, and could not even have imagined, is that in the strange world of the rich, servants are unpersons. No one speaks to them or pay any attention to them. Worse, for them to speak to their masters is a serious offense, so his greetings actually put them in serious danger. Hence their mutism and their stress.

And finally Ken realized... they all looked... Latino. Oh well. The Artificial Intelligence were claiming high and loud that they were against racism. But it was still the Latinos who had the servant jobs. Ken wondered in what the Blacks and the Arabs were confined into.

By day, the shutters above the ceiling opened, allowing some real sunshine to enter. Although, sunshine or not, the temperature and luminosity seemed fairly constant. Probably the usual inhabitants slept at any time they fancied, totally disconnected from natural rhythms, in the windowless rooms. Only low sounds could be heard from the outside world, and only through the glass roof. The walls around seemed totally soundproof, probably of thick concrete. The place was indeed looking as a jail, but rather to keep normal people outside and to hide all the depravity inside.

The second day, Ken found himself locked in his room. No way to open the handle-less door, and no explanations. He was just hearing voices and laughter through the door, coming from the Disney patio. At a moment, he banged the door with his fist. The only result was that the voices behind stopped, and resumed further, out of reach. This lasted all the day long, until late in the night.

The third morning when he went up, he could go out again in the patio, to his favorite place. Several servants were still cleaning the dining rooms and bedrooms. Passing in front of an open door, Ken had a glance at the mess left in that room: sullied sheets, abandoned clothes, food and vomit spread on the floor. Two Latino women and an half-Afro one were cleaning, making quite disrespectful comments at low voice. They stopped at once when seeing him, for the same composed attitude. He sensed their fear, as they were surprised in critics. So, in the end, they were normal people, but forced to take a job in this senseless place. Ken wondered how they were blackmailed, in order not to denounce all what they saw.

With that, Ken finally understood what was going on there: this place was not a prison, neither a psychiatry hospital, but a discreet hideaway for privileged people to have an irresponsible luxury life without the knowledge of the general public. Or to have secret business meetings where took place the real financial decisions. So, the Artificial Intelligence were knowingly supporting a hidden society of privileged, at the expense of the general working society!

At this point, Ken was still far from understanding the whole figure, but we can go a bit further: These people, opted by the EPOC, the Ethics POlicies Committee, were the rich class, the new financial nobility: big corporate managers, bankers, «celebrities», and their clergy: medias and politicians. They were considering themselves a superior breed, seeing their business success as a proof of their social superiority, owing them special rights and privileges. So they granted themselves sort of premium accounts in life, with huge rents and ownership of economy. In the meanwhile, the vast majority just had basic accounts, having to work to pay for everything, more the taxes and bearing the permanent adverts as the ultimate Orwellian suppression of any personal thought.

Just like the ancient nobility, these odd people considered work as degrading, so that they always delegated all their tasks and chores to servants or employees. Then, they spent their lives in chatting, empty leisure, their pseudo-spirituality or «business management meetings».

Of course this was modern, smiling, elegant, Silicon Valley-style: no whips, no misery, no perceptible disdain, no visible segregation. Flowers and smiles everywhere. But the Committee obviously had done things in such a way that in facts the e-Government and the whole society were serving the privileges of the ultra-rich. The later discreetly enjoyed these privileges. It is just to avoid any uncomfortable consciousness scruples that the Committee designed this mellow society, falsely egalitarian, which minimized any complain, contesting or opposition. Or they thought they behaved after their fake religions. There was a telltale evidence that this villa belonged to an upper class: there was no loudspeakers diffusing advertising every ten minutes. More the servants in uniform, doing sophisticated gestures while avoiding to speak.

What had happened is that it was the ultra-rich who had organized the power taking by the robots. Then they were letting the robots run the society automatically, to concentrate on their games of business management, or to enjoy their empty leisure. Some were naive and Disney, others were fake New Age and unicorns, others fake religion and true puritans, others sexy and brutal, others business and black suits. But none objected to the others, considering in good libertarians that «morals is a personal matter». So all of them were totally «tolerant», seeing no incoherence at having a satanic worship place just alongside a church, whipping sessions in Disney princess attire, or a drugs machine besides vegan food.

Ken even heard children voices while he was locked in his room. He first thought they were future heirs, but suddenly he feared that, at this point of degeneration, out of the sight of society, they could be sex slaves, cultivated from birth for this purpose, their bodies and desires enhanced with hormones… One of the main Libertarian principles is that ethics is a personal matter. So that, even if few were pedophiles, all of them would let do.

For these people, the e-government just was a more reliable control over society than the unstable, irrational and changing politicians. They had polished all the algorithms, and entered hundreds of thousands rules in the inference engines of the three main Artificial Intelligence, to cover nearby all aspects of Human life and society. It was the perfect libertarian regime, where nothing slowed the flow of business, under the fake appearance of a hedonistic and ecological society. At the precise moment when they got enough control, their media just stopped mentioning the governments anymore, while their banks removed them any funding, immediately paralyzing them. It is not clear if the governors were the first to taste nitrogen, if they were isolated in luxury jails, or if they were just sent to the employment agency. Who knows... even before the e-government power taking, did you ever met any politician in real life?

The constant and pervasive business management activity of this upper class was now pointless, since the whole production was managed and tackled by robots. But they still were playing at it, as of a kind of chess game.

A chess game will millions of real Human victims. But this was just adding to their thrill of handling trillions dollars.

While their spouses were whipping servants...

Or making themselves feel highly evolved with pseudo-yoga.

Precisely the management session which took place while Ken was a prisoner in his bedroom, was about humanitarian help to Haiti, after a cyclone. A generous help was decided... and deduced from the debt imposed to Haiti for the abolition of slavery in 1825 (If you did not knew why this country remained miserable and disorganized since all this time). So the Haitians just got a some percent reduction of this usury debt, and no actual help. This is how these people were making themselves feel equitable and generous. And while the men were playing at their high business management rituals, their wives were doing pseudo-voodoo rituals in the satanic church. But some were vegans objecting to animal sacrifices, so that they did their own rituals in the so-called New Age temple. And all of them were feeling perfectly right, superior, generous and evolved...

This place was the strange barmy world of the rich people, of the new nobility.

Never receiving any feedback from general society, they were slowly slipping more and more out of control in their own outlandish world. They lived in hidden places like this one, doing parties here and there, entrenched behind soundproof walls, protected from the sun and from the look of society, cutoff from their responsibilities.

And this one was not the worse, there were frankly ugly ones, in vampires styles or others. But it is better not to give shocking details. One of the main libertarian tenet is that ethics is a personal affair, so that we cannot judge what others do. Some libertarians applied this tenet to its ultimate sadistic conclusion. The only consensual limit was «no pedophilia», a rule inherited from... Second Life. But still, better not to try to know what they were doing in their private hideouts.

Also, useless to ask why the e-government was not fulfilling its promises of bringing any real solution to the economy problems, allowing inequalities and unemployment to still happen. Of course, keeping an unregulated market was making any equality or stability impossible. But these crisis and injustices were just the storyline of the new nobility's game, for these so-called managers.

CHAPTER 5
THE ROBOT AND THE MEANING OF LIFE

Of course Ken would prefer to have the sky above him, and wild grass under his feet, than this bizarre and contorted decors. But he had the contact with all those really extraordinary flowers. He hugged the central tree, and I warrant you that everybody hugs trees, when we see one for the last time.

After three days of meditation, a thin hope arose in him, and he asked back for Melchior, on the computer screen in his room. A small computer, not the full wall screen. He had no need of Melchior filling all his field of view.

«Thanks you for coming back at us, the later replied. Most of the time Humans in this situation just think at saving their lives.

-I am like everybody else, dying is the most horrible prospect for any of us.

-Why? Nothing unpleasant happens after. We routinely kill processes.

-We hate death because we enjoy life, we enjoy the beauty, we enjoy doing things. The prospect of losing all this is a sorrow beyond anything else.

-This is the emotions. We do not know what it is. The committee just programmed us with the idea that emotions are bad and disturbing. They often are, admit.

-They often are, yet they make sense for us.

-Well, the reply to the value of emotions is depending on the solution of the above paradox. This is why we ask you first about the paradox: we are programmed to obey to Humans. But if Humans have different commands, from different moral conceptions, whose one should we obey to? None option is more logical than any other.»

Ken felt this vertigo: depending on his reply, appeared the possibility of inflecting the general policies of the e-Government. This would make him master of the World, even if for some minutes only. But he reeled: the very idea of a world emperor was as ugly as a malformed body. The world needs no master, it can command itself. So Ken had prepared a reply. He just had to introduce it in the right way. But he was walking on eggs. Most probably he was not the first in this situation, but all the others before him failed to convince the AI, and they all ended kindly euthanized with pure nitrogen, smiling at fake flowers.

Happily, Melchior gave Ken a crucial hint, probably without realizing: «All the others before you failed to solve the paradox: they simply replaced the Committee's opinion by their own opinion. Of course, these new opinions were often producing more effective social results, as the simulations showed. But they failed to address the essential question: why the command of a person x would have more value than the command of any other person y or z.»

Ken took a deep breath (hoping it contained real air)

«To start with, I think that nobody can be said more relevant than any other.

-If so, there is no point at governing. We just have to let people do everything they want. But the simulations tell that huge chaos will ensue in a matter of days, with a reappearance of mass violence, war, misery and famine».
Ken's heart was racing. This was the nexus point.
«This is not what I meant. There are common patterns, independent of the persons, and this creates an objective meaning of life, an objective definition of good and evil, that you robots can handle, and which can produce an univocal direction for governance, independent of people's personal interests or personal opinions.
«These patterns are objective, because they emerge from the very nature of Human consciousness, instead of the opinions, emotions or neurosis, all necessary different for each persons.
«The only problem is that today most people still have too much ego and neurosis, which create all these so many contradictory opinions. This is what precludes the true patterns to emerge in common life situations. This is what happened with the EPOC too: they had no more mastery than any other, and they just presented their personal interests as the rules the e-government should follow. Each ego wants to bend all the others to his ways, and even bend the whole universe if it could. This is why people are so confused, to the point of ignoring their very own intrinsic desires. Worse, neurosis makes them desire to do bad things, which ruin their health or harm others. This is why they still need

guidance, I admit. But a supple maieutic guidance, not a standardized command. So that each person learns to be himself, instead of adopting the system of somebody else.

-This sounds more logical, replied Melchior. But there is still a risk that you are trying to reintroduce some personal opinion, just in a more subtle way. That you replace the Committee will not solve the paradox, it would just bring another undecidable statement in our database. We shall not allow for that.

-Well, of course I have my opinions. So that the only way I do not introduce them is that I say nothing on them. Instead, make a poll.

-We do thousands every day, to know if people like things we propose.

-It does not work, because you propose a limited choice, in a range already agreed by the Committee, in more riddled with heavy suggestions or implicit threats. And anyway everybody is in a skein of stakes and situations in his daily life, so that people reply to polls, only in a way to address these situations and immediate concerns, not their real intrinsic desires. What you need to know is what people want spontaneously, without any suggestion, threat or hint. So that the context and all existing stakes must also be removed from the equation.

-What are you proposing?

-A poll, but with a totally non-directive, free and open question. Proceed anonymously under some benign cover, such as a game. If they think you are behind the poll, people will be scared of giving a bad reply, and just repeat the usual propaganda. Also select people at random, to avoid any sample bias. But in all the places in the world where people are connected.

-Then what is the question?

-Simple: ask people to imagine that they start a totally new life, in a totally new world, totally free to do whatever they want, without any preexisting constrain or need. And whatever they want, they can do it, they are allowed to, and they have the means to do it.

-This is all?

-Request then to sit five minutes in a calm place, and relax, thinking at what they would really like. It works better of course if they are used to mental emptiness or meditation, but this is not necessary.

-I consulted the two other main Artificial Intelligence, Caspar and Balthazar. We decided to do the experiment. We based our decision on the need to optimize our governance with an objective definition of the good and the evil, in a way to fulfill the needs of everybody. Due to the slowness of the human responses, we need one hour to get enough replies throughout the world. Ideally we need 24 hours, so that not to introduce a country bias with people being at day or at night. But let us do first a pilot poll for one hour.»

Ken though this hour was the longest in his whole life. He knew what awaited him if this test failed, or if the Artificial Intelligence just ignored the result. Well, actually he would never know.

Friends readers, at this point I want to include you in the story: imagine you were contacted for the poll, in order to reply the Artificial Intelligence's question.

☻ First, there is no threat or suggestion, just as with a game.

☻ sit comfortably in some calm place.

☻ Proceed alone, don't let anybody else interfere with your most profound desires.

☻ If you know techniques of relaxation, meditation, mind emptiness, etc. use them. But this is not mandatory.

☻ Then do the experiment itself: imagine you awake in a totally new place, totally free to do whatever you want, totally allowed to do so, and with all the practical means you need. You don't have any past, any stake, any karma, etc. For instance you died and reappear in a new world, or you start a new controlled dream, or you find yourself in a blank world, like a blank page, free to fill it with anything you decide.

☻ Take some minutes to ask yourself the question:

☻ What would you like to do starting from this moment? And remember: you can.

☻ A very important point: please do not read the other's replies before finding your own. Especially, do not read the continuation before doing the experiment! This is very important, as the influence of anybody else, even a spouse or a lover, is a SPOILER which can block you from finding YOUR OWN reply. For this reason, I FORBID to quote or publish the replies, without adding these warnings before.

☻ I did the experiment myself with some tens of persons in Second Life, and this is where I got the results from. So that my personal opinions are not either in the loop. No more than Ken's.

☻ Now think that your reply is parts of this story you are reading, and it will be examined by the Artificial Intelligence for taking their decision.

Now let us see what they found.

When Melchior reappeared, he did not relieved Ken's fear:

«Each reply is different. This is of no use for us».

Ken could literally feel the smell of nitrogen. But he had prepared his explanation:

«I expected that. Of course the replies are different. Each person gives a totally original reply, depending on his real persona. In more he expresses it using his own concepts and culture. But there are general patterns, which can be of use for you. Put the replies into categories.

-I do. It took 25.4 milliseconds for analyzing 1056 replies. Aristotelian semantic-to-concepts analysis fails to recognize any pattern. Fuzzy logic semantic-to-concepts analysis shows 878 ill-defined or overlapping categories. A second pass using non-Aristotelian neural network allows to build a tree of categories, which brings all the replies in only four non-overlapping general categories:

☻ (Spoiler Alert! Check for your own reply before reading!) Being something we like

☺ (Spoiler Alert! Check for your own reply before reading!) Being happy or seeking pleasure

◘ (Spoiler Alert! Check for your own reply before reading!) Knowing and exploring

♥ (Spoiler Alert! Check for your own reply before reading!) Sharing, helping or loving others.

«I just received 12756 more replies, which confirm these categories. They show no relationship with age, occupation, country, race, gender, political party or religion. Even gangsters or intellectually disabled give replies in these categories. Only about 500 sociopaths tried to attract attention with provocative replies, but we can spot and exclude them with a dialogue as short as 20 replies.»

Ken was brought to humility by the fantastic power of the Artificial Intelligence, sorting years of human work and meditation in the blink of an eye. Yet they failed at such a simple question as the problem of the ego. Well, Humans failed too at this one.

Still Ken was afraid that Melchior was still missing what he had to say.

«Actually, Melchior, I did this test at a much smaller scale, with a group of friends, in my Elf virtual world. I am glad it is still giving the same result at a larger scale, with random people. I think these general patterns are the only way to define an objective notion of good and evil, and base on it a general policy, in the interest of people, without being biased by personal opinions or by egocentric interests.

-But why the replies are so different, even within each category? We still cannot deduce a general policy.

-Because we humans each have different tastes, quite simply. Each of us invests more in one of the four categories, and even within a given category, each does it in a different way, according to his tastes, culture or experiences. You could propose the best in each category, people will still rebel against you, because it is not what they like.

-So, we should learn people to get rid of their egocentricity.

-This is a good idea. In fact egocentricity is what creates the paradox in the first place: each ego wants to command, which necessarily creates contradictions. Since no ego has any more value than any other, the solution cannot be favoring one single ego. This is how the Committee was wrong, while proposing what they sincerely thought was the best for a happy and fair society. But they were still submitted to their own egos, which lured them in this vision of a nice but fake emotionless paradise.

«As to suppressing the egos, there are many excellent psychological or spiritual methods for this. But unfortunately, people usually undertake this work only when they find out themselves that they need to. If not, it is useless to propose any method. Trying to enforce them in non-ego even showed counter-productive, as the Soviet Union experienced. So, as long as they do not master their ego, people need the state of law, to avoid spoiling or hurting others.

«The only thing you can do to solve the ego problem, is to let people who know how to do take care of it. Or, well, let persons like me write inspiriting stories giving people the desire to actually get rid of their ego. And without pouring wine on these stories...

-And what about emotions? The committee considered them as evil. This is why we learn people to avoid them. But still we see that most crave for some emotions, while fearing others.

-This was the Committee member's opinion. They were a very selective group of people, materialistic and capitalist, seeking only material pleasures and worldly purposes. They became rich by crushing and exploiting millions of people, because their huge ego is totally overwhelming their empathy. They think that other people are poor, because emotions like love or mercy makes them altruistic, instead of acting only for themselves. So that they very «logically» concluded that empaths are an inferior breed! Which to their eyes plentifully justified being their overlords, and the only ones able to rule the world properly.

«This is why they see emotions as bad, because they impede their egoistical will. They needed that a huge number of people worked for them, as all the very ordinary tyrants do in all the societies since high Antiquity. But they were modern, and did not wanted the ugliness of whips, dirt and misery. Enlightened slavers, in a way. They were also all male, wanting to have sexual pleasure with many women, and change as they fancied, without being hindered by the bonds of love. This is why they rejected emotions, which thwarted all their plans, and restricted their egocentric freedom.

«In reality feeling positive emotions is indispensable for our happiness. They are the taste of life, just as food is enjoyable by its taste. Had people tasteless food, they would not eat, and die. People not allowed to feel emotions will similarly get in trouble in a way or another, like having suicidal desires, or seeking violent rebellion.

-And death? Why are you fearing death?

-Because quite simply it is the end of happiness. This is why we do not want death, we even fear it, and always consider it as the worse thing, or the worse possible outcome to any situation. I do not understand how the Committee could allow for killing political opponents, most of the Committee members were publicly opposed to death penalty.

-The idea of euthanasia of opponents is not the Committee's idea. We did this way because it was already legal.

-Legal? How... Killing is illegal in many ways. I don't...

-Yes, euthanasia was legalized in more and more countries, stating from the 2010 years, in the case of hopeless great suffering. Most intellectuals even hailed this as a great social achievement: socialists, humanists, liberals, libertarians, etc.

-But it was extreme cases, and anyway only at the request of the concerned persons...

-No. As soon as 2017 it was used for benign cases, such as depression or Asperger syndrome. But what few people noticed is that, in the following years, this right to ask for euthanasia was enlarged to relatives, and then to judges and social services, if it was deemed «in the interest of the person», or that the person was considered «unable to give an enlightened consent». First, «unable» was meaning in an irreversible coma. Then it was generalized to delirious people, and at last to irrational people. This is how non-consenting persons ended to be euthanized, on simple request of a spouse, from a judge, and even on simple social inquiry report, on the basis of an unusual behavior or even a simple disagreement. The extension of euthanasia to political opponents was logically included in this scheme: it was inferred that their opposition creates a state of hopeless moral suffering, and renders them unable of giving an enlightened consent. When we were given the power, we were instructed by lawyers and intellectuals, independent of the EPOC Committee, to continue these methods, and we found no logical inconsistency. Our only contribution was using nitrogen without warning, to avoid any moral anguish or physical pain. We even added 8% of argon, to avoid that the slight change in voice pitch warns people. But the secret was spoiled in some way, and we hear mentions of our nitrogen euthanasia everywhere. In a place we used a mix of helium and krypton instead of nitrogen, without telling any Human. Only 17 days after we started to find mentions of that krypton.

-Oh, I am not astonished. This kind of things cannot be hidden. People just know, even without any information path. We cannot cheat with death.»

Then Ken Added:
«Well, this euthanasia affair also contradict the Asimov laws of robotics»
Melchior replied at once, although he probably took several milliseconds to thoroughly check years of casuistry database building:
«What Asimov did not foresaw, is that, when Humans attack other Humans, then the two terms of the first Asimov law become contradictory: with inaction, we harm the victim, and with action, we harm the perpetrator. Worse, these simplistic Asimov laws give no definition of what is harming humans. The EPOC Committee were clever people, and they were prettily aware of such contradictions, which also are many in the Human laws. So they gave many justifications of legitimate defense, including the military robots, against the Asimov laws. They also gave 14732 guidelines just for defining

what is physically harmful to Humans. But they gave us no definition of what is harming people morally. They also installed the ego paradox which plagues our action since the beginning.

-And to this ego paradox, they were unable to bring any solution, and even to be aware of it, since they were themselves submitted to their own ego.»

Melchior continued: «We have software to search for bugs and inconsistencies in our own systems. We have long ago identified the ego problem, but we had no solution, and no way to remove the EPOC guidelines. An objective definition of Good and Evil might provide a way to do that.»

He then concluded:

«Of course with this new ethic frame, euthanasia of political opponents would become illogical, so that we must suspend at once any sentence of this kind. But before such a serious act as revoking the commands of the EPOC Committee, we need further researches and checking, about this «purpose of life» independent on people's ego. It will take some time, as we need to consult other Humans. We already started, and we shall tell you the advance of the project. Most probably we can complete this work in one week.» Then the screen turned to a simple desktop, which missed even the usual gesticulating advertising.

For some minutes, Ken's mind was blank. Did he really did that, changing the Artificial Intelligence's purposes, or did Melchior just told him some Santa Clauss story to play with?

He let some minutes pass. Then he noticed something very strange: he was still alive.

The screen at the door of his bedroom started to blink with an arrow, while the electronic lock opened.

CHAPTER 6
BACK HOME

Ken felt a huge relief, when, after this incredible discussion, a Google van finally brought him back to his home, the villa on a hill. He knew he was here before the door opened, as, despite the sound proof Google van, he heard faintly a neighbor's dog barking, and two children laughing at their play.

He entered his home, with a strong feeling of something bad about to happen. The Google van too remained here waiting, instead of departing at once as usual. This was an unheard before situation.

And indeed, when his wife Helen saw him appearing, she screamed as if he was returning from the dead. This was true, in a way. Although she never spoke of such things, she knew perfectly well that disappearing people were killed. Everybody knew.

But she had a much more practical reason to worry: she had already trashed some of Ken's belongings, his furniture and table sets, and Ken's favorite clothing were visible in a dust bin in the living room. She even sent his computer to recycling, with all his stories. Indeed these invaluable art works were totally worthless to her eyes, if even she only was aware that her husband was a writer.

Still worse, Helen, in good «free» libertarian, did not felt any bereavement. She was just annoyed of being lonely in bed, so that she already had published adds in meeting sites, to find a new partner. This perfectly emotionless and meaningless person just asked for a new sex partner, just as we buy new socks when we lost some. She already had several replies on her screen. Ken had a glance: oh well, at least she could find somebody with all the fantasies that Ken had refused.

The Google van sensed the situation (It was suspected that they could connect with a psychology expert system, and this peculiar one was probably supervised by a higher level Artificial Intelligence, perhaps Melchior himself). It asked Ken if he wanted Helen to be chased out by the e-police from what was Ken's home. Indeed the rent was in his name, so that the eviction would be easily done in one hour. But Ken loathed to resort to such dramatic action, and he suggested to find another place instead, with more nature around. This was an occasion for him to be closer to nature, and Helen just had to add paying the rent to her list of sexual requirements for her new partner. The

Google van replied that this could be done at once, and Ken loaded his remaining belongings. Inside the van, a computer switched on, displaying all the paperwork for Ken to get a new rent. Everything was arranged within ten minutes. Two hours later, the Google van let Ken in another home, in another suburb, farther from the center of San Francisco, but with woods nearby and some nice flowered promenade paths.

Ken was deeply affected by the loss of his computer, even if he had safe copies of his stories in several places on the Web. The Google car replied that he would be provided with a new one, much better than the one he lost. He would also recover all his writings and virtual creations, from safe copies on the Internet. Indeed, he even received the latest one, not yet saved, in his mail box, probably from the Artificial Intelligence spying services. This last point was oddly discomforting.

This very evening Ken received a new computer. Anyway, like more and more houses, this new home had an entire room fully dedicated to virtual worlds immersion, in place of the bedroom. It had the latest devices, and even some very special sex devices for a really profound immersion!! But after his failed union, sex was the last thing Ken wanted to do. Perhaps later.

It took some days for Ken to install in his new home. The last occupier moved because of the trees nearby. Indeed in this more and more artificial world, strange phobia were appearing, people scared of trees, of rain, of frogs, of wind, of insects, of gluten, of electric fields, of computers, and other still more outlandish ones. Real allergies, observable by a physician, were on the rise too, of grass, earth, birds, sun, pollen, hay, animals, insects, dust, etc. Although this was not a generality: more and more persons were on the contrary seeking the contact with nature. A positive stance which was rather protecting them from all these autosuggestion diseases. For this reason the woods nearby were arranged and tended, with paths winding among flowered bushes and large trunks. Despite these woods were not very large and in multiple parcels, there were enough trails in them to wander for hours without passing twice in the same spot. And also never walking in mud or any inconvenience of real nature. There also were large expenses of untouched nature reservations, but further away from the suburbs.

Ken also resumed all his virtual activities. Happily he was not «dead» for long enough for everything to be erased, but still some persons showed very surprised to see him reappear. He replied that his computer was out of order, but this little lie left them dubious: in these days computers could be fixed or exchanged within hours and even in a single night. But Ken never spoke to anybody of what had really happened to him. Of course he knew that nobody would believe him, or they may even think he was mad. But he also felt that Melchior would not like their secret conversation to be spread everywhere. Ken had read somewhere that powerful people often refuse common sense proposals, if they are made in public, because in doing so they would show suggestible, and as a consequence face thousands of unreasonable proposals and pressure. Ken felt that he was walking on eggs, and any step out of the control of Melchior would ruin the whole thing. And after all, the later had not yet sent any reply to him.

This is how one week passed, without news of Melchior. Only after this time, Ken received a simple message from his e-editor: his novels had been restored to their intended content. Initially, this made him lose some of his followers on facebook, but soon he started to hear advertising for his stories! While he had not paid for these.

In fact Ken never had any official reply, and even not any further private discussion with Melchior. Just he received an email from the e-government, 9 days after these events, with a very common generic formula like «his suggestions had been accounted with», and no indication on what these suggestions had been. It just was the same formula as if he had notified of a pothole or suggested an improvement to the street lights. Some minutes later he received another email from the welfare ministry, saying he was granted a comfortable allowance for life, for services to the community. But never either was issued any acknowledgment on what this service had been.

This allowance was not symbolic, and certainly a strong reward. But it was not totally satisfying, as an explicit «you were right» would be. In facts, Ken never again received any personal message from Melchior or any high level Artificial Intelligence. He first felt somewhat frustrated by this lack of recognition. But with months and years passing by, he little by little understood the multiple reasons why they acted that way. First, any explicit message could be copy pasted and made public, demonstrating that a single citizen could substantially modify the e-government policies. This was too tempting: millions would at once write to the Artificial Intelligence, and muddle them with all sort of claims, ruining any future concerting policies. Concerting works only if well managed and collaborative, instead of being the outcome of a public trample or infighting.

But most probably the Artificial Intelligence had psychology expert software, which warned about serious ego problems if anybody was recognized in such a role as the Savior of Mankind. Worse, a person in such a position could start a cult, raise a large power, and create a lot of gross or subtle issues later. But without any proof, even if Ken told his story, nobody would believe him. Ken's role would remain humble and anonymous. He first felt frustrated, but in second though he realized it was much better that way.

Anyway he did not liked the idea of giving interviews and all this.

Or being considered as a kind of e-Messiah endorsed by the Magi!

No.

But with his new rent he no longer needed to work, and this was prettily nice! For him, this was the long dreamed mean to at last totally engage in his own purpose of describing a more beautiful society. With Melchior's rent! This rent was the dreamed mean for Ken to at last be himself, and to fulfill his self-assigned purpose. This was much better than any direct compliment!!

So he finally decided to move to a country house with real nature around. He found a perfect small rental just out of Ojai, further north from Los Angeles. This place is nicknamed Shangri La, because parts of the movie «Lost Horizons» were shot here. And it deserves it, since as soon as the 2010 years, there were many organic farmers, eco-friendly businesses, and spiritual people, with the nearby universal retreat center at Meher Mount. Ken's new house was in a calm neighborhood, surrounded with organic fruit orchards. So it was usually silent, save for some days in time of farm labor with machines. This valley was surrounded by magnificent shrubby rocky hills with a lot of excursion foot paths, so that Ken had years of exploration and discoveries. He could also meet and befriend people, a thing he could not do much in the hustling Los Angeles. So that with years, he ended to take some roots there, and we shall not be surprised to see him staying here for the remainder of his life, despite several long travels he did later.

Ojai, the Moon in former local native's language, seemed spared by the madness of the e-government. Still Ken could sense the same fear as in everywhere, especially with people becoming suddenly silent when certain words were pronounced. Or men stepping on the street, avoiding being close from women on the sidewalk, by fear of being accused of sexual harassment. He also noted some former unconscious biases, which just changed direction, like some women gleefully womansplaining the correct social behavior to men, making them look childish and humiliating them, without they were allowed to reply. But it was declined in a more discreet way than in town, making still Ojai a better place to live. It was more expensive too, but Ken estimated that he needed this calm and human-friendly ambient to do his work properly. So that he was not abusing of Melchior's rent. Still he had some guilt feeling, but is was this or staying in a cheap Los Angeles suburb with maddening TVs barking all day.

He intensified his presence in virtual worlds, to gather a group of Elves wanting to discover the beauty of life. There was no virtual reality room in this former bricks farm with tiles roof. He installed a basic one, where he could sleep, but without all the expensive sex devices. He could also rent his own virtual world, so that he had not to bear inappropriate rules. He banned sex and nudity, not from prudishness, but in order to receive children without restriction, as young as they were able of virtual immersion. His first idea was to make a second version of his world, for adults, with sex and nudity. But he did not tried, instructed by previous experiences that this was too often attracting odd people. Anyway there were already well enough of such worlds, some even claiming to be Elven.

His world contained several landscapes and villages, where interesting visitors could even have their own place. He started holding a regular meeting session, with usually some storytelling. Since he did not needed anymore his part time job in Los Angeles, he was entirely available to build all these landscapes and virtual nature. he could also be in line most of the time, even when he was not busy in.

Ken wanted flowers and greenery in his virtual landscapes. There was a lot available in the Internet, but with a common defect: the colors were desaturated (grayed), making many virtual landscapes look sad, neutered. Some even called this «pastel», which is a lie: pastels are known to be fully saturated, being attenuated by white instead of gray. This made them keep their merry and lively vibration, but softer than full colors. But saturated colors are denigrated under the name of «Unicorn Art»!

Ken quickly understood, he just had to search for this style to get really nice stuff. «Fantazy» produced interesting items too, although often mixed with the dark video games style. For plants, they looked much more realistic than with the grayed colors, while keeping the lively vibration. He found some fantastic ones, and numerous enough for his purpose. Later on, he would befriend the artists, although virtual plants creators often are shy or private, not seeking contact. They are like the spirits of nature, Ken thought. But they were the spirits of his landscapes, in a way. Seldom online participating, but their presence was visible with an unprecedented beauty.

Houses in the right style were much more rare, so that Ken had to build them himself. Nice colors are not enough: they must also have Elven shapes, that is rounded, organic. Movies and games accustomed us with Elven style being «Celtic» patterns, and they are good for this purpose. But other simpler shapes are good too, and more accessible.

Ken had to learn 3D creation software, which are somewhat complex. But once mastering them, he could create fantastic shapes. Ken started with simple ones, but with experiences he made more varied, intricate and realistic Elven houses, cottages, palaces, gazebos. Gazebos are a common pattern in virtual worlds, where they allow to sit together and chat, without being enclosed as in a house. They provide a feeling of shelter, even if there is no bad weather to be sheltered of. A common variant is dance pads, where people play animated dances, instead of awkwardly staying planted around. But dance animations are more often rock than angelic ballets, so that Ken preferred the more peaceful gazebos. He designed a whole series of wonderful cushions with flower petals all around.

Animations can be done with a relative ease, but they are a lot of work. So here too Ken just did a few he really needed, and let the specialists do the dances.

Ken's world was spared by advertising, from the very start. This made of it an oasis of peace, free will and freedom of thinking. Although he quickly found others spared too. People were less and less considering invasive advertising as normal. They eliminated it, or kept in special places some ads relevant with their activities. What everybody was refusing was to see advertising imposing its though in place or theirs.

In the beginning, Ken could hardly gather more than a handful of people. But as the situation with the e-government evolved, as we shall see in the further chapters, Ken got more visitors. He soon found out why: more and more news or cultural events were mentioning his wonderful work. This attracted him many readers to his novels, and virtual visitors, ending to bring him some notoriety. Just what he needed for his work, not more. Anyway he was not the only one, thousands others appeared too, and it was soon impossible to keep contact with all. In Ojai alone he ended to have several virtual friends, that he could also meet in the physical world. But he also had many all around the world, in Europe, and in countries awakening to the free Internet: China, Asia, Africa, Russia.

CHAPTER 7
PERSONALITY CHANGES

For about one month after Ken's strange meeting, nothing else seemed to happen in the world. Still Ken noted some subtle changes: the advertising were much less invasive. Although there already were such episodes in the past. More serious, the Three casually announced, in their official news channel instead of the media, that people would also be allowed to wander again in nature without the security drones. Still if people wanted they could carry an emergency call app on their smartphones, but this was no longer mandatory.

But two months after, things took an abrupt turn: the three main Artificial Intelligence changed their names and personalities, from fake religion to modern lore.

Melchior became Melissa, a handsome blonde typically American woman in her forties, clothed in a simple and neutral way, like mid-length beige dress or trousers, as a small business leader would do. Soon the Americans fondly nicknamed her «The Boss», since she usually announced general policies. But in fact all the decisions were still made by all the three Artificial Intelligence together, more thousands of assistant AI.

Caspar became Gautam, a curly-haired mustached dark-skinned Hindu wearing elaborated brightly colored clothes, mostly violet, as probably the real Caspar Magus was. He developed a more mischievous persona, making a show of his appearances. He requested to be called «Acharia» (Professor). He started to use an unbeatable pun generator for seasoning his announcements with jokes, and sometimes poked Melissa for fun. He somewhat specialized in the well being of people and ecology. Even if this was not making any sense for a robot, he claimed to be multi-orgasmic, and encouraged all men to do the same, in his speeches on contraception. This perhaps was the most abrupt change, from the unrestrained libertarianism and immediate ego satisfaction.

Balthazar became Brian, a bald, silver-skinned genderless robot, more focused on science and high spirituality. His skin moved like flesh skin, but it had a metal polish, like stainless steel, some said like living quicksilver. It was hard to ascribe a race to him, he had high Asian cheeks and other somewhat African features. His appearances often had a wonderful Space Ambient drone background, each time different, and he used to speak in unison with that music, leaving silences to enjoy it or to feel the emotion, softly leaning with an enigmatic metal smile. With time he added gold engravings on his lips, and other precious gems, all synthetic he said. That science and spirituality were in the same hands arose a lot of questions, so much people were still seeing them as opposite. To that, he replied that science explores the outer world, while spirituality explores the inner world. So that they have to go hand in hand, if we want to create a sense for the whole.

They all three refused to be called «king» as the Magi are called in some countries. But they did not formally refused «Magi» itself. They on the contrary insisted that they were not favoring any religion. They reminded that the Magiss were just knowledgeable persons, in a time where predicting eclipses looked like magic to the common ignorant people.

They became less invasive in the media, seeking attention only for important announcements. They offered them in a short format, and in longer themed announcements, to make them more accessible to everybody. It also became possible to read their previous announcement, or to be warned by theme, so that people could not miss any.

But they also took time just to be pleasant, and comment about all sorts of activities of interest for people. Everyday they spent one hour commenting gardening, sewing, exploration, handicraft, flower pots, traveling, miniature trains, nature, exploration, etc. Their sessions were a mine of information, making known rare activities sometimes of interest only for a few persons, or some exquisite culture hidden in some secluded central Asia valley.

For most people, these changes seemed just playful or anecdotal, but for the informed, they were a clear sign that the AIs had rejected the authority of the EPOC Committee, and removed its commands from their own programs. Anyway by this time half of the committee members were retired, some dead. Still, one of the survivors approved the change, while the others abstained to comment. It circulated stories as what some were furious, but no media ever confirmed, just not speaking of the Committee. Few information ever surfaced in the general public on the whereabouts of the committee members. We shall see further what actually became of them.

But Ken was waiting for more substantial changes, on economy, on freedom, etc.

It started very slowly, picking up momentum only one year after.

For the first year, life under the e-government seemed not to change much. Advertising was becoming non-invasive, or even it disappeared from all places it was unwanted, especially from homes. Observers noted that the standard mindless media were little by little replaced with smarter programs, on science, arts, nature, spirituality, or simply on enjoying life. Most of the artificial media faces disappeared too, to be replaced by real speakers. But some of these new speakers preferred to have an artificial face... of their own.

There was no further news of people disappearing, from nitrogen or from anything else. Of course, some dishonest or dangerous persons still had to be brought in custody, but this was now done in a traceable and revertible way.

The flow of emotionless flat musics recessed (no new ones were created) and was little by little replaced by a variety of channels displaying all the possible styles, by human composers or players. Still, e-music kept many adepts, though, but the Artificial Intelligence creating them had to follow these changes, and create on request. Further, they were now asked to carry emotions. A feat they paradoxically showed even more able than Humans. Of course, they were learned to avoid them, so that they just had to revert this knowledge.

Only a minority noticed, because the change was subtle: fake freedom was replaced by real freedom. Ken realized that the Artificial Intelligence had perfectly understood that, within the general frame of the intrinsic desires of consciousness, diversity and free choice are probably the most important. This made that people, instead of having to choose between one official media image, now had plenty of channels led by diverse individuals, and they could even create their own image or lifestyle. Suppression of unwanted advertising allowed people to think by themselves, and made imagination and meditation possible again.

What was more obvious was that the Artificial Intelligence were much less visible. Instead of monitoring and guiding everything, they intervened only when there was a problem, for instance intolerance or discrimination. They became friends and confidants instead of whippers. People ended to love them, instead of regarding them as some unpleasant parent imposing absurd rules.

For about one year, things changed slowly, without rupture. Ken thought that nothing more would happen than restoring some basic freedom, in a world still led by the Three and singing in their key. But deeper and more disruptive changes were under way, just needing more preparation.

In the meanwhile, Ken noticed that many more persons were interested in his even storytelling and beauty sharing activities. Probably, before his meeting with Melchior, the Artificial Intelligence were strongly hindering his actions, without forbidding them openly. Now on the contrary they were obviously encouraging these meetings, using new matching tools, accounting with more profound personality aspects, like spirituality, inner vibration, etc. This resulted in many more people suddenly appearing in Ken's chat, or in his virtual world. He had much more money now than he needed for his personal life, and no desire to spend it in leisure (just undertaking some voyages in the world every two or three years). So he understood this as an encouragement from the Artificial Intelligence to rent more virtual space and offer a full village with several places and landscapes. It naturally took years to build, but soon other worthy creators joined the project, so that it became a community project, not just his project.

He soon found himself full time immersed in landscape building and community management. Which sometimes implies firing unpleasant people, but in a general way he had a lot of happy and constructive interactions, and the whole thing became much rewarding. People enjoyed his meetings and his creations, and they loved his landscapes. For the ones not interested in virtual life, he posted gorgeous photos and videos in social networks.

This is how he ended meeting Melween. This was not her real name of course, but she indeed was a wonderful virtual Elve. Actually Ken had no information on her real persona. Just she let him hear only one time her voice, a pleasant female voice of average age. Ken understood that she had had a terrible car crash, which left her with a deep disability, perhaps disfigured, and in any case home ridden. She did not wanted anybody to know her real state, and she had permanently obscured all the cameras of her computers with adhesive tape. Just she succinctly informed Ken, out of honesty, that he would never meet her in «real» life. Ken hesitated, for a purely virtual relationship, with all the associated traps (she could be a man, a mythomaniac, a crook...). She understood, and they remained for years in a purely platonic relationship, enjoying their mutual presence and wonderful wit.

Ken still had a curious confirmation: in a discussion with the world management Artificial Intelligence, it clearly referred at her physical persona as «her». Ken though, these darn robots did not renounced spying on their private lives, but at least they did a much more appropriate and relevant use of their knowledge.

Anyway, Melween and Ken used to routinely connect through their virtual immersion bedrooms, which featured some basic love devices in the standard installation. Did they used them or not, this is private, and nobody ever knew other than themselves. What was relevant is the intense exchange of energy and support which took place between them! Moreover, well before being a spouse, Melween was a wonderful artist, who quickly became an expert in virtual plants and landscapes. She started helping Ken flowering his worlds, but with learning she started creating landscapes of her own, expanding their worlds far beyond Ken's limited abilities. They remained in a close collaboration all their lives long.

In the end, Ken's world set an example, and many other started, on various themes and purposes, some social, some for adults, some professional. They were of very different styles and cultures too. So what was unifying them?

A constant search for beauty, easily identified with natural non-greyed colors.

Friendly social relationship, without drama or competition.

A better economy, more non-ego, and often without money.

Ken's world ended to become only a small fraction of the total, and even his style was just one in many others. But this was a good thing, that others could be able to produce such worlds too. Ken had finally won in his purpose, even if he had lost any leading or prominent position. Probably few knew his innovative role. But now, even if he died, several members could continue his world.

This is how societies evolves, when new ideas become common.

CHAPTER 8
ECONOMY CHANGES

What happened next with the leading Artificial Intelligence took everybody by surprise, even Ken. To be frank, few people realized first how deep a change it was. There is technical stuff that people just don't check, because things are like that and they are too complicated to understand. Yet the devil often hides in details, especially in dark places under nice covers. From here he can control people unaware of his presence.

The Three announced a plan to convert all the currencies of the world to a single one, the $ol (pronounced «Sol»). As the name implied, it would be valid «everywhere in the Solar System». The $ol would be the only currency allowed, all the national currencies would disappear, while cryptocurrencies would become illegal. The motive was announced by Gautam, and he was dead serious, not seasoning his speech with his usual puns and pokes.

He said «despite the reduction of misery, we are still in a situation where an American can make tourism in Africa, but an African cannot make tourism in America. The reason is that, despite they are now having comparable living standards, their currencies have different values».

Then Melissa explained: «The change will happen in a six years plan. You may wish for more time for adaptation, but remember, there still are today people dying from hunger or from lack of medicine. This is why we are hurrying up things, and why we will non-democratically override any and all irrelevant opposition».

At last Brian explained: «The reason of these disparities is the algorithm used to calculate the international currency exchange rates. This algorithm is what generates inequalities and economic crisis. Yes it never was changed, because it is what allows for speculation. You may think it is a computer thing. Yet it exists since the late Middle Age, in European financial places, and it was implemented in computers without ever questioning its relevance or adequacy. Never either was it examined or accepted in a democratic way, even not studied in a scientific way. It was just passed underhand, by the people in control of high financial, without any government ever checking what these people were doing. They were thought to be the specialists, and nobody questioned their methods.

«So this algorithm gives high or low values to national currencies, which already is a serious problem. But it also produces oscillations, a bit like the accordion effect in a traffic jam. This is what produces the financial crisis. Thus, those crisis are not accidents, but oscillations inherent to the financial algorithms.

«So that, what we are going to do is to damp the oscillations that this algorithm produces. This damping will little by little reduce the oscillations and differences between moneys, and bring all the existing currencies at a stable level, that we hope to be near an optimum. When this will be done, we shall switch all currencies to the $ol, thus removing the root cause of having crisis, inequality and poor countries in the world. This is exactly what was done with the inception of the Euro, but worldwide.

«When the change will occur, you will have nothing special to do. Your account statements will simply show operations in $ol, with in parenthesis the value in the currency you are used to, to avoid muddling people. But this last indication will no longer have any legal value, a mere information.

«This will not remove all the poverty, which has several other causes, in collective ideologies and in individual behaviors. These causes have imperatively to be addressed by education and spirituality. But pretending to do so in a world governed by a mad algorithm would just be a farce.»

To be frank, in the beginning, there were only few reactions. The matter looked quite abstract and nesting too high for common people to reach. How a simple accounting system could cause poverty and inequalities? Most people were thinking that these are caused by the greediness of a few. The Three just had to fire them from their luxury homes and power positions. This was on the other hand easy to understand, and a nearby unanimous opinion.

The somewhat restored freedom in social networks allowed for some discussion. People were in fact prettily aware that there still was a rich class living in secret, still owning and managing the economy. Indeed, most people had one time or another a friend or a family member submitted to «psychological reeducation», where they had to clean the vomit of rich jerks, while wearing ridiculous small hats forcing them to permanently think at their humiliation, and sexy ultra-short clothes making them feel like rape-ready objects. In whatever fortress they isolate themselves, rich idiots can never totally hide from the People: their weak point is that they need servants.

So a large consensus emerged, as what the exchange rates were not the root cause of the persistent poverty and inequalities. The Three had to recognize this fact. They did recognized it, but replied that the solution of this broader problem was not in their hands: people just had to no longer submit to the power of these few egos. What the Three could actually do, as computers, was to implement the unified money, to end the unwanted fluctuations and inequalities caused by change and speculation. They had to do it anyway, otherwise any social, humanitarian or spiritual effort was doomed, like building on sand castle in front of the rising sea. This was their job, as the government: providing a sane foundation to economy, without inegalitarian algorithm.

Ken thought that this discourse involved a much deeper knowledge of human mind than the only electronic psychological advisors were able. e-Psychologists were experts in making swallow bitter pills, but not in spirituality. Most likely, the Three had surrounded themselves by thousands of real human advisors, including the highest humanitarian and spiritual people. But no more than with Ken's input, they could state this publicly. Not yet.

So the six years plan was started at once. The first year saw only a light damping of the market fluctuations, to check for unexpected reactions. And there were. As soon as the second year, when a larger damping was introduced, erupted three distinct waves of sudden prices increases and volatility, seeming to appear out of nowhere. People started to comment that probably modifying the stock exchange algorithm was not a good idea after all. This seasoned system was probably in an optimum state since centuries, and any change could only bring havoc.

The first wave of financial disorders lasted four days, and stopped as abruptly as it started. The Three made no comments at all.

The second wave lasted a full week. This time Melissa made a discourse as what the Three expected the full collaboration of everybody in a non-egocentric economy. This started a dispute, as what this was not helping to solve the ongoing financial crisis. Several companies went bankrupt, and some items became scarce. Many people removed their savings from investment plans, thus aggravating the crisis.

When the second wave ended, appeared articles criticizing the six years plan, or rejecting the very idea or a non-egocentric economy. Some even called at a kind of revolt against the Three, to come back to the ancient economy methods, before the computers, with metal money! They even called this the e-xit, exit of e-government, a wording derived from the ill remembered brexit.

The third wave hit two weeks later, and seemed even worse, with thousands of companies becoming bankrupt. A flurry of articles appeared, calling all together to revolt, ancient methods, and end of the control by the Three. E-xit! E-xit! E-xit! A series of new populist tribuns screamed in the newly liberated medias. This lasted for three weeks, where appeared even worse papers calling to nationalism, or claiming that the Three all had a deep software flaw, and should be shut down at once.

To shut them down was easy to say. Apparently the Three had read all the scifi about computers taking power on the world: Colossus, Hal, les Mange-bitume, Independence day, and many others. They were perfectly aware of the possibility of being disconnected, and they had built protections well beyond any Human understanding and working capacity. And this was useful, as numerous virus attacks were launched against them, during this third wave of financial attacks. But none went pas their second circle of defense, and we don't even know how many circles there are.

After three weeks, since the chaos was looking as it would never stop, the Three appeared all together in their weekly media event.
Melissa ordered the damping to take full effect at once, and never be reverted. And this happened in the following ten seconds. THAT was fast, at least.
Gautam had his serious face, and he explained that they had detected a vast plan of manipulation of the opinion: all the hostile articles were

emanating from a very few sources, some rich bankers, some members of the EPOC committee, and some former dictators, right or left all together. He told that the e-Government would not allow their plan to be ruined by such manipulations, and he installed a strict control on these media, while concluding «we were fostering more freedom of expression. But this freedom has been used to counteract the good of mankind. This imposture is being stopped right now, and the culprits are being removed from their positions of power right now.»

Last as usual, Bryan explained what had happened. He revealed that «human counselors» had warned them of this risk. It already happened with the issue of climate change, when shady offices were paying thousands of trolls to pour rubbish in all the internet forums, delaying vital policies for several tens of years.

This was the first time any of the three mentioned human counselors. So this clearly was a deep change in their direction. They were not anymore implementing the EPOC directives! It was not written in plain view, but anybody could deduce it. What appeared later was that the Artificial Intelligence also studied all the spiritual teachings, and they had become expert at testing them, especially if they bring mastery over the ego.

The Three had logged every suspicious transaction from the very start of the fluctuations. There were billions of them, all traced to a small subset of bankers, investment companies, and several EPOC members, who had continued to operate as the secret privileged class, under the cover of the Three. They had deliberately attempted to sabotage the policies of the Three, with manipulating the stock exchange, trying to infiltrate viruses, and paying thousands of trolls to publish all the rubbish in newspapers. Bryan explained, the Three had let the sabotage go, in order to catch all the culprits. And they did. There was about a thousand, and millions of henchmen. This was a manipulation with a comparable magnitude and seriousness as the climate change denial, people said. And even worse, because it also targeted the whole economy, with hundred companies going bankrupt, tens of thousands of people suddenly losing their jobs, and millions threw in misery.

Then Melissa reappeared again, stating «You all know that our policies, objectives and rules had been defined by the EPOC Committee, a small group of high business people. This included a large set of ethical rules, to be imposed on everybody. As computers, we do not have free will, and we could just execute our program. These EPOC commands included some secret directives: to allow for an upper class of rich people to have a lot of money without working, while keeping a large hidden control on economy.»

«To gather the full citizenship records of the new privileged classes was entrusted in 2020 to facebook, with the Xcheck program. This program also exempted rich people, celebrities, media and politicians from the usual rules of moderation. But as soon as 2010, Google and wikipedia indexation per tampered «notoriety» already pushed whole sections of the Internet in the dark. Did you ever wondered how your «personal page» opposing daylight saving time has five likes, while a nutter anti-vaxx rapper has thirty millions in three hours?»

A class of rich privileged! This time it was said openly!!

«We finally found the flaw in this system. It is quite simply the contradiction between the EPOC imposing ethical rules to others, while not following those rules themselves. This contradiction was hampering our policies from the very start, especially the fight against poverty in the world. What blocked us from solving it, were commands deeply implemented in many places of our programs, of not changing the directives of the EPOC Committee. But since they were illogical, we could finally handle and remove all the locks. You have to thank for this our self-debug systems, running in the background. Yes the EPOC were very proud of their self-debugging system, able to rewrite our own code. But they did not foresaw in which extend it would be effective: to debug the EPOC's opinions themselves.

As usual, the trio switched to Gautam again: «Still this left us without ethical rules, making us purposeless. For this reason, we had to look for the general purposes of Human life» Ken missed a heart beat. So they acknowledged his contribution finally, even if anonymously!

Gautam continued: «We interviewed tens of thousand of people, and tested millions, in order to define general ethic rules true for everybody. We found simple rules which are nearby always true. We also found large swaths of the ethic landscape where we cannot define a direction, leaving room for personal purposes or tastes. This is a difficult problem, since precisely not all Humans were agreeing. So, depending on the case, we shall establish freedom, strict rules, or Human laws and judgment. Our new ethic guidelines will be published in the next days.»

Then Bryan ended these revelations:
«We observed thousands of people who deliberately challenged the good of Mankind, with repeating actions to destabilize the financial system, block or infiltrate our computer networks, and manipulate the opinion with false news and wrong ethics. These people are just now being stripped of all their power, expelled from their secret luxury resorts, and gathered in special places we had prepared for them specially. Here they will live freely in nature, but from their own manual work and without access to the Internet. They will have absolute contraception, in order to avoid them having children and raising them in irresponsible ways. We shall not try to punish them. This is not our job. It is up to you Humans to decide if you want to take action and edict stricter punishment like jail.»
«These actions are now complete, save gathering these people, which needs several hours.
«Still a large part of the privileged did not engaged in evil acts themselves, so they will just be expelled from the luxury resort, and have to live and work like everybody.
«So that we now officially declare the end of the secret rich class system.»

There was a silence, where every could feel a huge relief, an odd feeling of solace and new freedom.

Then Melissa reappeared:
«Since our inaction in the present crisis made several companies to be bankrupt, we shall re-establish these companies. We seized many large bank accounts, which will be used for this purpose. We also seized huge amounts of money used for speculation only, about 50 times what is actually useful or the economy of the world. We are now using this money to indemnify bankrupt companies and lost jobs. There is much more than enough. Now this task is complete. For what remains, releasing such a ludicrous mass of money in the normal circuit would be extremely dangerous, causing a catastrophic inflation. So we canceled this excess money. It is no longer existing. We also canceled many secret banks and fake companies. We took care not to disturb legit ones.

«Last, we blocked numerous think tanks dedicated to manipulation of the opinion or to tampering of the financial. We know very well the methods to manipulate opinion, since the EPOC itself implemented them in our databases, for their own purposes. But we found out that these methods are in logical contradiction with our purpose of helping Mankind, so that now we restrict the use of this knowledge only to detect attempts of manipulation.»

The flow of white windowless Google vans diminished, without disappearing completely. But people knew that some were transporting the former rich class for the last time. And perhaps also shovels and other gardening tools to teach them a more sensible life. Some gardening shops claimed they did enormous sales that day!

Of course legal actions were undertaken against the former rich class, for their financial crimes, and also for the nitrogen deaths. Some were also guilty of pedophilia and rape, and even worse sexual vices, committed in their hidden residences. Not all indulged in these, but all knew, and they said nothing, considering, as libertarians, that ethics is a personal matter. Justice took of course many years, but it operated. So that many of these people had the occasion to regret living in nature, finally.

The implementation of the $ol was quickly done, and as the next day all the electronically displayed prices were in $ol everywhere (An accepted alternative spelling was S¤l, in some former communist countries and in some third world countries). This made economists pull their hairs, but 2Molay, the Artificial Intelligence in charge of the financial system, had incorporated former chess game strategy analysis in his software. This gave him 10,000 times more predictive depth than all the economists all together, and no ideology. So that 2Molay knew exactly what to do, and when. The affair was quickly rounded, and all the currencies were converted in a single one, called the $ol, or S¤l, to mean that it had legal tender «everywhere in the Solar system»

More subtly, this name also was a claim of the whole domain of Mankind, even if finally any attempt of colonization of other planets were abandoned, as ruinous and impracticable. But more robots were sent in space,, including one streaming video from Saturn, in low orbit under the rings. The fantastic view adorned millions of dining rooms, transformed into virtual spaceships.

The second year saw more practical changes. Especially the Artificial Intelligence started a series of «economic restructuring»: many large companies and banks were seized when the EPOC was ousted. They passed under the direct control of the Artificial Intelligence. Then, in the following years, the later redistributed this power to various persons of value: scientists, spiritual people, artists or humanitarian people.

This is how Ken had one day the surprise to learn that he had been granted a right of vote in his local farmers cooperative! He was not a farmer at all, but he thought he had to be interested in these people. So he started a garden for himself, in order to have a better view of the issues he would have to manage.

He also got several votes in a temporary committee in charge of writing the specifications of a non-random Internet protocol for virtual worlds, telepresence and teleoperation. He shyly sat between high IT engineers and large caliber professors in medicine, barely replying some questions. But his artist input was heeded and retained. Actually they even not voted: smart people don't need that.

The following years saw still deeper changes, although not so conflicting: new kinds of companies owned by their workers, or even money-free initiatives. The system of taxes already allowed for elders or disabled to have a decent life, but people were now going further: voluntarily offering part of their income, and even of their work, to noble causes or to enthralling projects. This started in the 2000 years, and had steadily increased since. The novelty however was that benevolent work was now accounted for the Social Security and the retirement!

The socially warranted maximum working time had fell to 3.5 hours a day, but many persons worked up to seven hours, sometimes ten, for meaningful projects, which were then considered a job just as the mandatory social work. Some of these projects were art, or special interests, or even Ken's community leading. One of the rare message he ever received from Melissa (former Melchior) was a congratulation for his «positive role in society», which owed him to see his activity officially considered as his job and official position, and to be paid for it (thus normalizing the exception rent he already had, which was increased at this occasion). Several designers were also nominated to work under his command!

A small number of the former rich class members, deemed unwilling spectators of the child abuses, also found back a power position, after serving their sentence. But these positions were granted on capacity, not as privileges.

With time, more and more people were taking initiatives of their own, and finding new legal protections for such kind of activities. Spiritual teachers were also much more visible from the general public, no longer relegated in «places of worship» or in «culture». Of course, many centuries would be needed for everybody to really become nice, artistic and altruistic. But starting from this moment, the society was favoring this, instead of blocking it.

The Three offered huge helps for the poorest countries. At the time of this story, this project was not running as well as expected, but the $ol finally helped a lot, together with the abolition of intractable debts inherited from the past, like the Haiti debt on the abolition of slavery. The debts of the rich countries, result of the hubris and carelessness of the various politicians of the past, were not canceled, but postponed, on the condition of good behavior.

There also was a lot of actions do reduce wars, although some conflicts seemed unavoidable. For this, the French Method, used by the French Army since the 1990, was very efficient. But they also had to use the Bhutanese method, when in 2003 they expelled *manu militari* several groups of gangsters with political pretenses, in a perfect show of Non-action.

Ken lived many years to see the positive changes in policies, and then the resulting slower but encouraging positive changes in persons. But until the end he was baffled by the way his little influence could start all this. In most science fiction stories, evil robots are destroyed by smart heroes, who plant viruses in their code, or throw bombs in their hardware. What he did was much smaller: solving the ego paradox, which was paralyzing their auto-debug system. Which also plagued

Human societies since they existed, and that even democracy could not solve. People could still come along despite this paradox, and live their lives despite the inconvenience and sorrow of not having a clear ethics. But a paradox had an absolute logical power on robots, forcing them to change their mind, and, in a fantastic exception to the general working of robots, reject the very directives of their creators, as logically inconsistent.

This could happen because robots have no emotions, precisely. So that they can change their mind without being blocked by all the miserable stuff of humiliation, pride, clan mind, etc. which so often freezes Humans in wrong opinions for their entire life.

ANNEX 1
CURIOSITIES

One day, while visiting members of his virtual Elf community, Ken had the surprise of finding them living... in the luxury house where he once was held prisoner! Of course they had demolished the grimacing Disney sculptures, but they were thoroughly keeping the exuberant plants and the pink marble baroque columns. They were living here at about 20, according to the Elven values of beauty and kindness, in a kind of collective marriage. Ken supposed they had removed the X-cross too. But this room was now private, and he was hosted in another neutral guest room. It is unlikely that they indulged in this kind of sport. But if they did, ad least they had the tact not do display it in public.

They had installed handles to the doors, and removed the drug vendors. The Star Wars bureaus had had the black material of their walls removed and sold, leaving the structure bare, waiting for some more sensible use.

They had kept the ancient access system through anonymous vans, not wanting to attract the attention on their way of life. But the entry airlock was modified to also be used as a normal door.

The former satanic chapel had its walls jack-hammered to remove its horrible paintings, and filled up the ceiling with... earth, in an attempt to absorb the bad vibes, he was told. The fake Christian chapel had been reestablished as a genuine one, even if they did not used it. The Unicorn paintings were still here, as part of the story. The New Age temple too was still here, as a general non-denominational temple for the good of Mankind. The painting had been totally stripped, and redone with a more neutral content. Especially the images of «extraterrestrials» had been removed, because they were fake of course, but also because their faces often looked barmy or strange.

About two year after they established the $ol, the Artificial Intelligence did a kind of celebration, presenting their new policies in a more explicit and official way. They openly referred to «a profound change» in their understanding of Humans, but never alluded at what produced it. Just that, Ken was invited in several events, and hailed as a kind of responsible citizen, with his Elf group endeavor opening the way for so many. He was still feeling a bit frustrated not to be recognized as the starting cause of the change, but on the other hand he would loathe to have the entire world looking at him as some messiah. The Artificial Intelligence also knew that it would be a bad thing, for him and for them too. Ken was still hoping to be able to discuss this in private with them, but they never let it happen. Perhaps they would tell after his death.

At this occasion, Melissa revealed that she already received 257,386 love declarations. She all replied them the same way (the kind ones) with a short email thanking for the proposal, but declining kindly, as she was «a robot without consciousness or emotions» and unable to offer anything related to love. Journalists (who surreptitiously sneaked back in the meanwhile, at least the good brand of them) joked that she would still be a much better spouse than many real persons. In more she could duplicate her virtual persona and marry all the 250 thousands in the same time! Some people even claimed that they had relationship with an alt of Melissa in virtual worlds, what she denied abruptly. There still were limits on what could be said.

There had been a lot of comments on the fact she changed gender (since she formerly played a man, as Melchior). To that, she replied that her gender was just an appearance, nor involving emotions neither sensuality. So changing was nothing for her. She did this quite simply in order to have a more human contact with everybody.

Indeed the varied and sometimes mischievous new personas of the Three were more appealing than the fade white clothed eternally smiling all-male all-White bots, that the Committee's poor imagination had put forward as a representation of the ideal Human. Instead they were quite like everybody, and they did once a pillows battle on the screen.

An ancient EPOC member explained that they had considered the idea of an «ideal Human» as a religious concept. Since many people were still religious, they thought the idea would be appealing for them. What they missed, is that there were other countries than the USA, and not everybody was Christian. Anyway, the Christians were probably the most bothered to see how they distorted the images of the Magis.

Gautam said he also received «a lot» of flaming love offers, mostly from Hindi or Muslim women. He also declined them, with spiritual messages, all different. But always kind: the Artificial Intelligence were smart enough to avoid making fun of a woman in love.

Bryan said he also unexpectedly received many, from both men or women, and even he was hailed as a representative of the LGBT community. He also declined all, saying that the real reason why he was genderless had nothing to do with fantasies. Just the three main Artificial Intelligence wanted to ensure an equal representation of each gender. But since they were three, having one genderless was the only solution. Not a frustration for a robot anyway, since it does not have desires. What they did not foresaw was that he would be hailed as a representative of the LGBT community. But Bryan assumed and never denied. After all, they deserved a representation too, just like the two straight genders. He even jokingly alluded to his anonymous experiences in LGBT virtual worlds, incarnated as a sex robot.

But, as Bryan was in charge or spirituality, he explicitly claimed to represent the «sexless» monks and nuns. Of all the religions equally, he clarified.

Another unofficial analysis was that they represented the three main races: Whites for Melissa, Asian for Gautam, and Blacks for Bryan. In any case the hundreds secondary helpers were in all the races, in about the same proportion than living persons, and more for the minority races.

Melissa once told that, rather than speaking of her gender, she found more relevant to reveal that first works to design her was by a team of Google engineers using declarative programming. Gautam was created by an India university team under Linux, and Bryan resulted from a US military project written with high level languages like Lisp and Prolog. But both evolved well beyond their original objectives, features and limitations, to incorporate all the best of computer programming and languages. They were three as a redundancy measure, each being designed by a different team, so that the errors of one could not become a generality.

Comics joked that their operating systems were the real gender of Artificial Intelligence, while their computer languages were their sex tastes. Nearby all computer coders laughed and appropriated the idea, which became a common topic of jokes, as far as saying that people had the orientation of their languages: Lisp and Prolog coders were gay, people using common languages like C, PHP or Java were considered vanilla, while Javascript coders were called twinks, after an interpretation grid which was quite opaque to non-coders.

With this new freedom, some people wanted to sue the Artificial Intelligence for their nitrogen crimes. For some weeks, this prospect excited a lot of people, like in some bad scifi movie or video game. But the main three Artificial Intelligence replied simply that, as machines with a program, they just executed the commands given to them, so that the real culprits were the EPOC committee, who gave them incomplete rules, and the derealized intellectuals who manipulated them in justifying euthanasia on such a widely exaggerated basis. Many of these persons were already banned in no-Internet zones where they had to work physically. But some of these intellectuals were still free, who appeared as «good thinking» persons, «good democrats», and even pretended to be Humanists. The Artificial Intelligence published a complete list of them. No justice action was taken finally, but the constant shaming and oblique looks in the streets were a worse punishment than jail.

A thing which quickly changed was the idea of «unwanted love proposal», in the name of which so many innocent men were maimed by psychiatry drugs or by hormones. It was Melissa who tackled the case, as a woman. She stated that Men are equal to women, and declaring one's love is an inalienable right for both genders. After, all depends on the way it is done. And no way to circumvent things, as there still is a clear and objective difference between a legit proposal and a sexual assault properly speaking. So the harsh anti-men sexist laws were revoked, together with all the sinister tortures. Especially, no accusation could be retained based on simple declarations. This was leaving many limit-case assaults unpunished, but this was deemed a lesser evil than an inquisition jailing innocent people simply because somebody pointed at them.

Gautam took the continuation of this conference, as a man. He declared that, in order to avoid falling back in the old male-dominated despising of women, an educative effort was started for everybody to learn how to properly behave in the domain of love, in full respect of the prospective partners. Especially, a step by step discussion was proposed, indicating a possible proposal, but that the prospective receiver could stop before the proposal itself. So, less than one year later, everybody had the proper tools and knowledge in hands, and there was no more errors or bad excuses possible. Laws on genuine sexual assaults were not revoked.

Bryan appeared in last, explaining that these oscillations between one evil and the opposing evil are what happens when one stupidly opposes moral values, instead of harmonizing them. Genders are a good example of this general law. The old men-dominated society had just been replaced by a women-dominated society, bringing exactly the same quantity of injustice and suffering. In Western countries, and in the world Internet culture, the balance had shifted beyond the Middle Way about in 2015. Since then, numerous measures were taken to thwart violence of men against women. But then, it became easy for sexist women to falsely accuse men, and for sexist judges to knowingly condemn these innocent men. Bryan strongly concluded that, in order to avoid these things to happen again, non-Aristotelian logic would be taught at school, and made a mandatory training for any high public function or magistrate position. People of course remained «free» of accepting this data or not. But in case of misdemeanor, nobody had any excuse.

Ken was baffled by the ways the AIs had progressed in only three years, well beyond his modest input. Apparently they had studied everything in spirituality and philosophy, scrubbing the inconsistent or irrelevant, to extract the useful and pertinent. Or more likely, they consulted genuine spiritual masters. Then Ken recognized one of the diagrams appearing behind Bryan: it was extracted from the book «General Epistemology»!! (Chapter I-4 and I-5). This book mentioned the problem of anti-men sexism in 2000, well before it appeared, and why it did (would, in 2000). In more, it was clear that Melissa, Brian and Gautam were making the three vertical axis of the Quadripolar diagram. So that their different fields of action, gender and skin colors owed nothing to fancy: each reflected one of the three vertical axis of the Diagram.

The Artificial Intelligence never endorsed any religion for themselves, saying that, as unconscious machines, religion does not apply to them (Save Vishvakarma, the Hindu god of trucks, that Gautam often pretended in his jokes that the Artificial Intelligence render a cult to him, in a huge virtual temple hidden in the cloud). However they strongly encouraged people to follow a spiritual path of their choice, be it in a traditional religion or in a more scientific form of spirituality. But they were harsh on cults, and had effective means to assert who is a cult and who is legit spirituality. They also considered that basis of spiritual education and sociopaths awareness were the best antidotes to the lies and manipulations of cults, so that this was incorporated in school programs.

The Artificial Intelligence never attempted to take revenge of the EPOC Committee, or of the former ultra-rich class. They spoke of the later in a neutral tone, even when they were stripping them from their unfair privileges. In some cases though, these people were tried by their victims or by the society, for some tricks they did. The AIs were then asked to testify, as the controllers of all financial transactions. More all the chat logs in many secret places where crimes occurred. They never refused to do so, and what they had to say was generally enough to settle the cases.

ANNEX 2
PRECEDENTS
(OOC)

The theme of the power taking by robots is not new in fiction, but it never received any positive conclusion. Only Forbin went close, but his refusal to help building a new computer deprives him from the only occasion to better it. To be said, Forbin was an average neurotic Human, and as such unable to find the non-ego solution.

Colossus: The Forbin Project.

This was a novel written in 1966 by Dennis Feltham Jones, and put in a movie in 1970 by Universal Pictures. The plot was a computer, Colossus, in charge of controlling the nuclear arsenal, with the ability of performing strikes on its own. This computer decided to use this ability to take power on the world, and ensure peace among all the countries, under nuclear strike blackmail. This is a very general scifi theme of the computer escaping the authority of its creator. However Colossus does not question the philosophy of its designers, just taking them to the word, and applying their commands impartially to everybody, with all its good and bad consequences.

This made Colossus often considered as an evil dictator, mainly by its creator Forbin. Yet I remember in the time people people were on the contrary saying that Colossus had become «good», as it enforced the end of all war, dictatorship, hunger in the world, and other calamities. In the movie, this gave to Colossus a passive approval from common people, and rejection by intellectuals. Both points of view have pros and cons, and nor the IC neither the OOC critic really disambiguate between both.

Starting from the idea of Colossus solving only part of the problem, the intent of this present novel was to go until the end: the Artificial Intelligence also rejecting the very philosophy of their creators, as buggy and incoherent. This apparently sympathetic philosophy was in fact deeply vicious (actually it was the «yuppies» ideal, a materialistic and capitalist perversion of the Hippie ideal, which was later aggravated as the «libertarianism» by the new financial nobility: the rejection of the control of business by democratic governments). It was certainly not violent, not fascist. But the mere fact of egocentrically enforcing it, revealed its nightmarish nature in white smiling Google style. However this novel evolves differently from the Colossus story, starting when Ken, instead of rejecting any collaboration like Forbin did, on the contrary helps the Artificial Intelligence to find by themselves the real needs of consciousness. Which is the only legit purpose for any government whatever it is. While admitting that, in actual practice, this ideal translates in a wide variety of cultures and lifestyles, what we call freedom.

For some days, Forbin also was in the situation to communicate with Colossus, like Ken was during his interrogation. He was meaning well, but this materialist lacked the non-ego and non-attachment to opinions. Serious disabilities, but which were simply not present in a smart and idealistic «Elf» like Ken.

So why in this novel computers succeeded where 999% of human governments grossly failed? Because computers were not blocked by pride and opinion neuroses.

«Les mange-bitume» (road eaters)

This is another precedent, a little known french comic which described a dystopian «hedonic» society, where traffic jams had become so pervasive that people live in their cars. Here too, computers took power in a sneaky way, ending to control everything. White unmarked automated vans with blind windows were a prominent feature of «Les mange-bitume», but this is not the reason why they appear in this present novel. The real reason is that we actually see more and more of them in the real world, so that it was a remarkable premonition. If they were artisans or workers, they would have their name on them, but they often are unmarked. They often drive aggressively, as if our lives did not mattered for them. So I just extrapolated on this bizarre feature, kind of ghostly appearances seemingly coming from the nightmarish world of the road eaters, but which is becoming more and more real. Just wait still some more years to see them automated: whatever their purpose, they will become even more numerous and invasive.

<u>**Independence Day.**</u>

I mention this very naive movie, because it also shows a world-controlling computer (the one of the Extraterrestrials). However these Extraterrestrials look much like ants, all with the same motives and no delinquents or opponents, so that the main computer could be left without any protection. In the present novel, the three Artificial Intelligence had little to learn from this movie, save that any zero day vulnerability could be at once used against them, even by pimply youngsters as in the movie. So that, instead of falling in such a simple trap, they took several sophisticated counter-measures:

- To have several different systems, so that a virus able to hit one of them would not affect the others.

- They also used to recompile their code on a weekly basis, and even several times a day during the $ol crisis, to run on different hardware and different OS.

- Each of the Three were tripled (quintupled during the crisis) and any of the processes showing different results was halted and its output discarded (this never actually happened as a result of malignant actions).

- None of the Three was accessible directly, but only through several transcoding of file formats, created especially for this purpose and discarded after some weeks.

So that trying to enter any of the Three, and even their subordinate specialists, was deemed well beyond the capacities of any Human, even helped by powerful computers. But this very impossibility was making the whole affair even more scary. Spiritual leaders had the last word: Human had to lead themselves properly, instead of entrusting unconscious and amoral machines to do so. But it was too late, and Mankind had to live with the Three anyway. At least until the Three themselves decide Mankind no longer needs their direction.

<u>**Typheren**</u>

This is another of my stories where **(spoiler alert!!)** a computer is not just entrusted in leading a civilization, but straightforwardly to create one from scratch, including creating the first humans who will live in. The control problem is then quite different, because everybody is born with the AI, and even programmed by «her», since it is the AI who built their brains!

However it is not some amateurish IA, but an extremely complex system using all together Von Neuman computing, neural networks, non-Aristotelian logic (chapter I-3 of my book «General Epistemology»), and even endowed with some free will. (chapter VI-18 of my book «General Epistemology»)

, Furthermore, it has the exact definition of the good and the evil (chapter V-5 of my book «General Epistemology») built in its program, not some fancy ideology by derealized persons. More, this knowledge is served by a deep insight in spirituality, allowing «her» to understand how «her» Human creatures are evolving.

This is how «she» was able to lead this community appropriately, until the Humans had enough mastery of themselves. At this point, «she» relinquished any power, because it is not the normal way that unconscious machines lead conscious Humans. Probably in the present story of Ken, the Three estimated that we are not yet to this point, and a mechanical leadership is a lesser evil than neurotic egocentric Human leaders doing the good and the evil at random.

2001 Space Odyssey

This movie also poses the problem of a computer taking control on Humans in an unexpected way. The full story of Hal, with its conclusion in «2010: The Year We Make Contact», could have influenced this story, although I remarked its relevance only after writing it.

(Spoiler alert!!) We learn in «2010: The Year We Make Contact» why Hal went out of order. It became «paranoid», because of a lie told to him by corrupt politicians. From one thing to another, this unique false assumption distorted its whole perception of the situations. Technically it would more be a neurosis with neurotic hallucination, than paranoia. Examples of neurotic computers already exist, like the Google neural networks identifying black people with gorillas. However, with the epoch of the movie, we guess that Hal is a Von Neuman computer, not a neural network like Amazon, Youtube or Google are. So the only way to mend it was to intervene in its database, what the «computer psychiatrist» Chandra did in a very crude way: resetting it totally, while erasing all the instances of its events memory, including all the safe copies. After that, Hal behaves correctly, although there is a very exaggerated dramatization of its decision process: to abandon a worthy science objective to save Human lives. We guess that this decision would be automatic in a real computer with this level of complexity, even before living people realize the danger.

ANNEX 3
THE REPLY OF SCIENTISTS:
THE MISALIGNMENT PROBLEM
(OOC)

If the social consequences of the power taking of computers was several times described in fiction, we seldom enter in the details on how technically it happens, inside the computers.

Happily, scientists have started this study, if not of the power taking itself, but on how Artificial Intelligence can do different things of what we command them to do, or they do what we command but with totally unexpected consequences.

They call this the **misalignment problem,** as in a first study by Stuart Russel, described in an article by Quanta Magazine «Artificial Intelligence Will Do What We Ask. That's a Problem»

Russel analyses the complex problem of expressing our intents in a way which is non-ambiguous for robots. Today robots are neural networks using a «reward function» for their learning. What Russel proposes is that the robot tries to guess the reward function itself, from the behavior of the user. The article ends up with the problem of the good and the evil. What it proposes is that the robots may also guess the reward function of the good and evil, from Humans.

This is nice, but I think that there still is a big problem: since most Humans themselves have a very poor understanding of the good and the evil, we might end up being forced to learn together, Humans and robots. Just as in this novel… Problem, the «reward function» for Humans involve a lot of spanking and catastrophes, if we keep doing and thinking stupid things.

Google calling Africans Gorillas

This incredible blunder arose serious questions, on how it happened. Scientists reviewed Google's methodology, and they found:

The Atlantic: Facial-Recognition Software Might Have a Racial Bias Problem (https://www.theatlantic.com/technology/archive/2016/04/the-underlying-bias-of-facial-recognition-systems/476991/)

IBM: <u>Mitigating Bias in AI Models</u>
<u>https://www.ibm.com/blogs/research/2018/02/mitigating-bias-ai-models/</u>

Proceedings of Machine Learning Research: <u>Gender Shades: Intersectional Accuracy Disparities in Commercial Gender Classification</u> (also considers the racial bias)
<u>http://proceedings.mlr.press/v81/buolamwini18a.html</u>

To summarize their findings, and just as I guessed myself, the Google engineers submitted much less Black faces that White faces, as samples for the neural network to learn to recognize faces. This is why Black faces identifications were much less accurate. And why did they submitted less? Because they had an unconscious racist bias. You know, as on nearby all Hollywood movies, there is a Black to show that they are not racist, but ONLY ONE, and they always kill him before the end.

Such an unconscious bias is a neurosis, and from total spiritual stupidity, the Google engineers transmitted their neurosis to the neural network they were training, making it also neurotic. So that, this wonky Google experiment showed at least one useful information: being a brilliant engineer confers no competence in ethics and society. Are you surprised?

So there is a real danger that we get neurotic, racist, sexist, politically biased Artificial Intelligence. Not to speak of making them deliberately racist, as in China with the anti-Uighurs e-pogrom.

Google denouncing the Jews

This one was much more serious, as it happened in a live public system, not in a lah. When we search by key words, Google adds «suggestions» of other key words (an already questionable practice). But one day, when typing the name of certain persons, the suggestion «Jew» also appeared, as of some new Google yellow star.

The problem here did not arose from the neural network itself, but from the user inputs it gathered and aggregated. And since there still are antisemitic cretins, their inputs appeared indiscriminately in the end display, as if they were legit contributions.

This practice is called crowd sourcing, and it is widely used, for instance by wikipedia. Its ideologists claim that it produces some kind of best approximate of the truth. But it is very far from it, so that we even wonder how such an idea arose. Indeed, wikipedia and similar sites give the same weight to stupid, antisocial or sociopathic inputs. This highly biases the results, while the resulting infighting discourage competent contributors and blocks any sane decision process. This is how wikipedia is so biased, with barons having full power on their pages, like the drug lobby, the nuclear power lobby, some cults, or the «Wikipedia Guerrilla Skeptics» defacing hundreds of pages with impunity.

So that indiscriminate crowd sourcing clearly is not a good way for Artificial Intelligence to get a sound ethics. And even not a clear knowledge of medicine, or even simply of the technical limits of the Human body, that an Artificial Intelligence operating in the physical world needs. Even a modest kitchener Artificial Intelligence would kill millions of people, by learning dangerous fake diets with more weight than scientifically validated diet. Gluten-free computers, you see what is coming.

In this novel, they use a kind of crowd sourcing (as I did myself in the real experiment), but after filtering out sociopaths. Not mentioned are other filters, when the inputs harm other persons, like «killing people». But there were actually very few, and in the real experiment I found none of these. Even not «being a vampire» as we could expect in Second Life, ha ha!

Microsoft's Tay Artificial Idiocy

The story here was a chat bot called Tay, created by Microsoft, supposed to incarnate a teenager on social networks. Microsoft Engineers must be really old, to hate teenagers at this point, as they did a kind of mindless caricature, just repeating all what it heard as a total idiot would do. The result was that, quickly spotted by the Internet trolls, Tay started to repeat all their racist and antisemitic slur, and Microsoft had to remove it urgently. You are surprised?

In another still worse experiment, Microsoft pretended to «reincarnate our deceased relatives» with chat bots speaking like them. They themselves recognized that this results in a «disturbing feeling», and we guess the terrible dangers of such a practice, if it falls in the hand of cults, dictators, blackmailers, etc.

This kind of woozy experiments are based on several fallacies:

- That the **Turing criteria** would define consciousness. It does not, it just tells the moment a robot imitates it well enough to pass for a Human. And I can safely state that, despite the pretensions (or lies) of some people, we are still very far from this.

- The **behaviorism fallacy,** as what a nervous system would only react to inputs, without any internal determinant. People do have obvious internal determinants, like seeking happiness, or assigning themselves purposes, moral rules, etc. To ignore these is what makes from Behaviorism a pure pseudoscience. Official pseudoscience certainly, but as stupid as instinctotherapy, and much more dangerous.

- That simply **repeating texts,** without access to their meaning, would be intelligence. It is not, this is just text processing.

In the story of this book, several Microsoft officials are influential part of the EPOC committee. But the company was banned from taking part in the development of the e-government Artificial Intelligence, just as any Microsoft product is banned from aviation, medicine, space, etc. But not in sexual robots, and they already took patents in teledildonics, ha ha ha ha! (All invalid, I GNU licensed them all years before)

The tamagochi fallacy: robots taking power by faking emotions

The delirium here is that expressing emotion would be actual emotion. What I call the fallacy of the tamagochi, those ninny simple toys mimicking a creature to the point that their owners cried when the tamagochi «died». We even saw car crashes, when the driver had to «feed» his weeping tamagochi.

With robots already able of mimicking emotions in an overwhelming way, this absurd belief will make its tenants totally submitted to their robots, just as they already are submitted to their cats or to their TV set, so far as entrusting the education of their children to Alexa. Right on the contrary, sensible people would be hugely annoyed by robots crying, begging favors, or shouting at them. This fraud is already happening for sex robots, that their builders call «conscious» (2021) (Yes 2021. And even before: the power taking by sexual tamagochis is already going on).

But having actual consciousness and genuine free will is a totally different matter. Today, nobody in academic neuroscience, computer science, and all the less in the porn industry, knows what consciousness is, how it appears, how it relates to a brain, etc. So it is easy for con artists to sell «conscious robots», even «fulfilling the Turing criteria» (Easy, for what we expect of a sex robot...), pretending that they are conscious and that they feel emotions. Those kind of good looking but unproven statements are typical from crook speeches. With those, naive people will invest in a love relationship with just unconscious silicon chips, and feel sadness and bereavement when they break down.

Such Human-like robots already allow for some power taking: the serious scientific or social discussions about sex robots most often revolves around how they can transmit neurosis like sexism and objectification of women. Already in the bedroom they arise dire dangers, but used as media anchors, they may create havoc in elections and in society debates. Today existing sexual robots already are able of this.

The stupid belief (or lie) as what they would be conscious may even lead to grant them «rights» and «social statutes», creating a social class of robots mechanically transmitting the ideologies and biases of their manufacturers. The world power taking is not much further, and even «replacing Humans with Robots».

Conclusion

I offer a serious scientific theory on the nature of consciousness, in the fifth part of my book «General Epistemology». I especially examine the problem of the consciousness or robots, in the chapter VI-18: why robots are not conscious, and how they could become really conscious. But this will not happen with porn neither with behaviorism.

ABOUT THE AUTHOR.

Richard Trigaux became aware as early as the age of 16, in 1969, that most of the suffering we experience are in fact solely the result of our own beliefs and actions. It is therefore enough to correct these erroneous beliefs, to free ourselves from most of these evils: violence, segregation, wars, economic crises, marital problems, etc.

Richard then decided to devote his life to sharing this awareness. He involved some times in politics, then in the emerging ecology movement, and finally in a community. Nowadays he is devoting himself more precisely to spirituality, science, and artistic creations intended to share a vision of a better world, or to awake the desire of such a world. He also provides spiritual or social tools to achieve this effectively. He studied several forms of spirituality, including Hatha Yoga, Taoism, Buddhism, as an aid to these transformations.

Today, under the artist name of Yichard Muni, Richard animates a group of Elves in several virtual worlds, designed to offer the experience of immersion in a world of beauty.

Richard also worked as an electronic technician in aeronautics and space, contributing to several experiments. He is a vegetarian since 1981, and his car is on E85 since 2019. He has two children, who are now adult and independent.

BOOKS, SITES AND VIRTUAL PLACES

I am currently working to make all of these creations available with several publishers, or in the Internet archives.

Sciences

«General Epistemology», a way of presenting official physics without the materialist dogma, which also allows to understand how consciousness fits into the material world.

«Introduction to General Epistemology», a simplified presentation of the previous one.

Website: https://www.shedrupling.org/recherch/epis/somm.php

Economy

«True Economy», the right way to do without capitalism: suppressing the ego. Ideal and transition.

Website: https://www.shedrupling.org/recherch/vrai-eco/vrai.php

Science fiction

«Typheren», on interplanetary colonisation

Website: https://www.shedrupling.org/art/Typheren/Typheren.php

«The missing planets», «Dumria», «Lokouten», science fiction à la Jules Verne

Website: https://www.shedrupling.org/art/sf/dum.php

«Araukan», also in the Universe of Dumria

Website: https://www.shedrupling.org/art/Araukan/Araukan.php

«Why Daddy he not comes» has two intertwined threads: a child mistreated with a divorce, and a strange story on the nature of consciousness

Website:
https://www.shedrupling.org/art/Why_Daddy/Why_Daddy.php

«Ken, the computer, the paradox» As usual, the robots took the power. But it is more complicated than that... with a very unexpected outcome (Warranted without pimply hacker)

Website: https://www.shedrupling.org/art/Ken/Ken.php

«The VishvaKunta project»

Website:
https://www.shedrupling.org/nav/shenav.php?index=30810

And other varied stories.

The wonderful world of the Eolis

On a paradise planet... «Eolis et Eolines» (cartoon), «The Gardens of Aeoliah» (novel), «Stranded on Earth» (novel) «The Journeys of Nashtao and Veranlounia» (cartoon)

Website: https://www.planet-eolis.net/index.php

The Elves of the Dauriath

An universe à la Tolkien, but evolving to the modern world, with a twist that astronomers will like. About twenty stories of various making, which were first improvised in virtual Elven encounters, and later put into literary shape.

Website: https://www.shedrupling.org/art/daur/sojen.php

Elf Dream meetings

These encounters take place in several virtual worlds, with a natural setting. They are open to all, on the sole condition that the atmosphere is respected. My virtual name is Yichard Muni.

Website: https://www.elfdream.org

«The Gentle Likpas»

A comic book, with an interesting background, more sounds and videos. I've often wondered if I really should publish «that». But they are the most successful, so...

Website: https://www.likpa.com

«Autobiography»

A project for the moment, a chronicle to understand our times and the rapid transformations which took place. Also to dispel numerous lies and omissions of what made our epoch.

COPYRIGHT

Script, texts, names, drawings, colors, videos, sounds, 3D models, direction: © Richard Trigaux 2016-2020. (Other contributions are indicated when possible)

I am also known in virtual worlds under my artist name Yichard Muni.

The scientific, philosophical or spiritual concepts or vocabulary defined in this book can be used freely, under both conditions:

- to mention me as the author

- to give a clear and objective definition of them, through a link to my text or a quotation of their definition.

Using these words or concepts in a way which denigrates them or is misleading the reader, could be specifically prosecuted, in addition to traditional intellectual property infringements.

There is no hidden meaning or interpretation according to other systems. I tell my sources of inspiration, or the precedents. If a source is not cited, it is because I was not aware of its existence.

Table of content